An Affair to Remember

By CC MacKenzie

To Matt!

Happy reading,

Christie

An Affair To Remember - Copyright

Published by More Press

Cover Design by *Gabrielle Prendergast*

Prologue

At the ripe old age of fourteen, for three long minutes, Marc Atelier died.

Lucky for him, a crack accident and emergency team at the London and Westminster hospital, some of whom had honed the skill of bringing back the dead in Afghanistan, kick-started his heart.

Twenty years later Marc donated his hefty bonus, Nico Ferranti was a very generous boss, to the hospital's outreach scheme, a scheme set up to help tackle gun and knife crime in the city's mean streets. The knife that had nearly killed him had been recovered, but the coward who'd stabbed him disappeared.

All Marc remembered of that night was a pain so hideous, like blades dipped in the fires of hell itself, piercing his lungs with every gasp of breath. He'd found himself sprawled face-down, unable to move, in a gutter awash with the worst human filth imaginable. Police sirens shrieked too loud in his ears as cars screeched to a halt. Then the sound of feet running, his own scream in his head as he was lifted by rough hands. And then darkness.

And all because he'd tried to put a halt to a gang initiation ceremony. The boy, Eddie, had been too young, ten, and the apple of his sixty-two year old Nan's eye. A woman who'd more than once filled Marc's empty belly and bought him second-hand sneakers that fit. When things were bat-shit crazy at home, the old woman had given him the battered couch he'd shared with a flatulent mongrel. On the night he'd been stabbed, Marc had managed to get Eddie away with strict instructions to run for home. Then he'd turned his attention to the trash who'd use a child to do his dirty work. The ensuing *discussion* had ended with a knife in Marc's chest. He shouldn't have tried to reason with a sixteen-year-old high on a cocktail of vodka and crack. Stupid. He'd been stupid even to try.

For days he'd hovered in a drug-induced fog on the sharp edge of the increasingly monotonic suck and beep of machines. Dimly aware of cool, gentle fingers taking the pulse at his wrist, a voice telling him he was going to live, that he'd been lucky, blessed.

When his eyes opened, could finally focus, he found a young Asian nurse with dark, kind eyes staring down at him, and a doctor with exhausted eyes who didn't look old enough to hold a razor.

He had tubes in his throat, up his nose, while bags of God-knew-what were pumping a cocktail of fluids and drugs into his system and he was so weak he couldn't lift his head.

Deep down inside him lived the real fear that he'd end up in a wheelchair, or worse, for the rest of his life.

"You're very fortunate to be alive," the doctor said.

Yeah, right. What the hell was the point of being alive?

How could he trust them when they told him he'd make a full recovery, when he didn't have the strength to lift a fucking finger, never mind take a take a leak on his own.

Two days later he was off the ventilator but not off the heart monitor.

The man who for days had sat like a ghost in the corner of Marc's room now rose from his chair. As he crossed the floor with a lazy stride, his police issue black boots squeaked on shiny linoleum the colour of a battle ship. The face of a grizzled warrior stared down at Marc. He heard the gruff-voiced police sergeant with penetrating eyes - eyes that seemed to easily read the terror in his - tell him he *was* lucky to be alive. Luckier still to have an A-one team of medics who'd brought him back from the dead. Those eyes and the don't-give-me-any-bullshit glare, seemed to cut right through Marc.

Then the sound of a disturbance in the hallway outside his room caused Marc's eyes to go wide and the machine that monitored his heart-rate bleeped faster. The shriek of a voice he knew too well made him squeeze his eyes tightly shut.

AN AFFAIR TO REMEMBER

Shitting fucking hell.

Her shrill voice echoed down the corridor, sounded more than pissed and not the angry kind.

The door was thrown open and a too skinny woman teetered into the room on too skinny heels made of eye wateringly pink plastic. Her hair, at least a week past the need for a wash, was the colour of musty straw. She was dressed head to toe in leopard skin lycra that did nothing for bony hips, a flat ass and an empty push-up bra. She looked like a woman who'd been on the game too long. She looked like a woman who'd fallen on hard times. She looked like a child's worst nightmare, which was nothing but the truth since the woman was Marc's mother. Kohl rimmed eyes, bloodshot, settled on the sight of her son laying on his back on the hospital bed. Those eyes slid over the tubes attached to every orifice including his dick and showed no emotion. Lulu Atelier (good name for a stripper) didn't even attempt to put on a show of motherly love or affection for the policeman now sitting at attention in the corner. Instead, she launched into a foul-mouthed rant. A rant Marc had heard every single day of his life.

"I've had the police at my door. Effing social services bitch has taken away my baby girl. See what you've done? You're a loser, just like the tosser who fekked me."

"Good for the effing social worker," Marc said, his voice hoarse and hurting. "Maybe the poor kid will have a chance."

Lulu's face was in his.

And Marc's nose wrinkled as he turned his head away from the breath-holding scent of fags, soiled clothes and old sex.

"You're out of my house, hear me? Out!"

"Whoopeefuckingdoo," Marc said to his mother's back as she attempted to walk in a straight line to the door.

And then there was silence.

A silence that was too loud in a room filled with the bleep of machines.

"So." The cop, dressed in black combats and a vest of a thousand pockets, folded his beefy arms and stretched out long legs. "You saved the boy, Eddie?"

Marc's response was to stare hard at the ceiling with burning eyes. "Maybe."

"My name's John Jones. Sergeant Jones to you. How about a brand-new start?"

Chapter One

From his state-of-the-art office in Ludlow Hall, Marc Atelier toggled an electronic mouse, checked the eighteen flat screens on the wall. It was a foul night, bitterly cold and wet. Even though the car parks were packed with everything from Ferraris, Porsches and Bentleys, Ludlow Hall was nice and quiet.

Two weeks before Christmas the hotel was full of yo-ho-ho cheer. The restaurants and bars crowded with guests. No sign of trouble. Movement on the fourth floor of the Tower Suites caught his attention. He let intelligent blue eyes linger on a young couple dressed for a party having a quick fumble as they waited for the elevator. The blonde had her hand on her date's groin just as the doors pinged open. Marc kept a weather eye on them in the elevator as the guy backed the blonde against the wall, his tongue titillating her tonsils while searching hands raced under her dress.

Marc had no idea what it was about elevators and lust, maybe it had something to do with a confined space and pheromones, but his security team always had elevator sex mentioned somewhere on the nightly reports.

Then his gaze dropped to movement in the up-market restaurant.

Marc's grin was wide as he kicked back in his chair, hands clasped behind his head and blew out a low whistle at the wondrous sight of one Elena Kennedy, head receptionist at Ludlow Hall, being led to an intimate nook. Elena was a stunning brunette, tall with legs up to her armpits. She had bumps and curves in all the right places. By the way her gorgeous hips were swaying in a black dress that could have been sprayed on, Elena was on a hot date and looking for action, baby. He wondered who the lucky bastard was. Marc eyed her escort and his dark brow rose in surprise. The one word he'd use to describe the guy was...

boring. Everything about him was medium. Medium height. Medium build. Mousy hair. Nice enough face. Then he frowned because her date looked... nervous. The guy's eyes were darting all over the place, refusing to land on Elena. An Elena who was adjusting the top of a dress with skinny straps. A dress that showcased fabulous breasts, not too big and not too small. Her tongue swiped over cherry red lips as she eyed her date as if he was going to be dessert with whipped cream and all the trimmings. Now the guy's fingers were running around the neck of his shirt. Marc didn't blame him, he was a little hot under the collar himself. The jolt in his groin made his mouth twist. He always had that reaction to Elena. She was outstanding at her job, ran her team with discipline but also a light touch. She was great with guests. And she was funny and completely irreverent to the senior staff, and that included Marc himself. Grinning at the way Elena was now flirting shamelessly with the head waiter and making him laugh, Marc got back to business.

These days Marc Atelier was head of Ferranti Security. A role that encompassed all of Nico Ferranti's interests. At the moment he was located at Ludlow Hall. Tonight he was doing a surprise inspection, camera angles, blind spots and on the eight night staff, hand picked by him.

Nico Ferranti had called him into Ludlow Hall from the Ferranti Hotel and Spa at Lake Como where Marc was based. Someone, a nasty little snitch, employed at Ludlow Hall was selling stories to the press. For the last six months little drips of information about Nico and Bronte Ferranti had appeared in the Tabitha Crew column in a down-market tabloid. Unpleasant, petty pieces sprinkled with a hint of the truth and then twisted. Little drips that could only have come from people who were close to the couple and their family.

So Marc was looking very closely at the staff, especially administration, housekeeping, reception and Nico's trusted personal assistant. The task might feel filthy but it had to be done. He'd found two bugs in Nico's office. One under his desk and one behind a picture frame. (Someone, Marc decided, had been watching too many Bond movies.) The bugs were still in situ.

AN AFFAIR TO REMEMBER

Meanwhile, three of Marc's best forensic techies were trawling through personal computers, analysing email traffic, including all personal data. Amazing the things people said on the Net and social media. But after four weeks, nothing had dinged.

But Marc Atelier was a patient man.

He'd fine the mole.

On a personal note, being back in the United Kingdom at Christmas couldn't have come at a better time. Because John Jones, the man he'd called Dad, the man who'd turned Marc inside out and made a real man out of a street kid, had died suddenly four short months ago. And the woman he now called Mum and Marc's twenty-year-old half-sister were still numb with grief. Hell, he was still numb with grief himself.

John and Mary Jones had changed his life twenty years ago, and the life of Marc's baby half-sister, Nina. The couple had walked into his hospital room and offered the choice of two paths to take, the right one or the wrong one. Marc had chosen the right path because he was clever enough to realise Sergeant John Jones might be better as a friend rather than an enemy. Going *home* was no longer an option. Thank God. Being a street-wise punk held no appeal after he'd been stabbed. Social Services agreed, if he ended up in the system, prison shone brightly in his future. A social worker with tired eyes had told him to grab the chance for a better future. With some mighty fine medications swimming through his blood, Marc found himself listening to a voice whispering in his ear to take the chance of a fresh start. He'd given the Jones' a narrow-eyed look and laughed them off as a couple of touchy feely do-gooders who wanted to do their bit for a better society. Fair enough. He'd chill until he was back on his feet and fighting fit. Apparently they had a home in Devon, a place which for a boy who was used to the bright lights of the big city, sounded like 'Middle Earth'. But a spell of the quiet life was just what he needed, for now.

The couple also told him they had... rules.

Okay.

Education, they stressed the point, was crucial.

Fair enough.

When he could be arsed turning up for school, Marc breezed through the work.

No alcohol.

Not a problem.

"No drugs," Mary said, in a steely voice that made Marc blink.

Maybe she wasn't as daft as she looked.

He gave her an angelic and deeply charismatic smile.

He could turn on a charm offensive when he felt like it.

"Never touch them," he'd said.

Which wasn't quite true. It was perfectly true he didn't take drugs himself. But he had handled them and been cautioned by the police for possession. And he was absolutely certain that if he needed some cash he'd be able to find a pusher to deal, even in a sleepy little hollow like Devon.

John Jones had been watching him like a steely-eyed hawk.

Then Mary sent Marc a thin smile that didn't reach her grey eyes, eyes as sharp as the blade that had slid between his ribs.

"You're a very pretty boy, Marc," she said now, her gaze penetrating through his skull to see right through to the bullshit. "You're also a thief, a chancer, a dealer and a clever liar. We're prepared to do our best to help you, you little twerp. So do not mess with us."

The corner of John's mouth jerked as if trying hard not to laugh.

He rose, placed a heavy hand on Marc's shoulder and squeezed.

"If I were you, I'd take her advice. Take it from me, son, she's not a woman to tussle with."

Three weeks later Marc found himself in the Jones' large family home on the edge of the Atlantic Ocean. And instead of taking off when he was healed, he'd found himself staying. Then, when six months later John and Mary had taken in his baby half-sister, too, Marc Atelier had found himself a family.

Now his father was dead, and at thirty-four Marc grieved deeply for the man who'd relentlessly pushed him through school, university, the marines and then in the police force as a senior

SWAT officer. And John had celebrated when Marc had accepted a career boost from Nico Ferranti. A man who'd immediately recognised a reformed bad-boy just like himself. No one from Marc's old world would recognise the boy in the smooth, sophisticated man who wore designer threads, silk tie, smart shoes of the finest Italian leather. A boy who'd been a gang member, opportunistic thief and drug dealer.

Marc knew John Jones had been fiercely proud of him. A fist of grief rose up into his throat as he remembered the day his father died. John had been sitting in a chair after walking the dog. He'd fallen asleep and never woken up. And just to compound the tragedy, the dog had died in its sleep two days later. Together the family had wept, at times they still did. Nina had told her brother in words of one syllable that she would not return to university until her mother was back on her feet. Pride rose through the grief. His sister was a beautiful looking girl, but more importantly, she had a great big heart. Family, she said, came first.

Now Marc was the man of the house. He'd come back to England for his mother. He'd come back for his sister, and he'd come back for Nico Ferranti, another man who'd changed his life.

Marc narrowed his eyes as he left grief behind. He focused now on the wall screens and the job at hand.

Someone was trying to cause mischief for the Ferranti's. And they'd gone to a great deal of trouble to set things up. Marc was good at his job. He had the skills, but more importantly the way to get inside the head of a criminal and to ask the right questions. And the first question to which he needed the answer was *why*? Why would a trusted member of staff betray a man like Nico? Money was the biggie. Next came revenge. So now Marc's fingers danced across the keyboard as he dug deep into the financial circumstances of the people closest to Nico Ferranti and then the people closest to them, moving out into a wider and more complex circle. It would take time. Something would turn up. It always did.

And all the while, Marc kept one eye on the wall screens.

Chapter Two

"You're a nice girl, Elena. But this relationship isn't working for me."

Elena stared at Tom and couldn't think of a single thing to say.

A voice was screaming in her head, he's *dumping* you. He's dumping you right in the middle of your workplace. How embarrassing was this?

And he's dumping you two weeks before Christmas.

Who does that sort of thing to a person?

And right on the heels of that thought came, why the hell hadn't she dumped him first?

To be honest, she'd only gone out with Tom in the first place to keep her brother Liam happy. Tom worked with Liam and her brother had told her in an earnest voice that Tom was a, "Lovely guy."

But Tom, Elena knew after their first date four weeks ago, wasn't her type.

Now she couldn't believe that she'd actually felt sorry for him.

Because here she was being *dumped*.

That'll teach her to pity date.

Tom was... boring.

There was no getting away from it.

Elena took a gulp of the vintage Chianti he'd ordered without asking her, nothing but the best for Tom, and tuned back into what he was saying.

"You can be amusing occasionally, too," he wittered on, oblivious to anyone and anything except the sound of his own voice. "To be honest." He took a deep breath. "I can't live with the no sex rule..."

Elena's thoughts screeched to an emergency stop.

Whoa.

AN AFFAIR TO REMEMBER

Just hang on there a minute, Tonto.

No sex rule?

What no sex rule?

Elena opened her mouth to discuss at length a rule that was, to put it mildly, news to her, when a disturbance at the entrance to the restaurant caught her attention.

Her eyes bugged in her head.

Omigod.

Quickly she dipped her head and focused on her blackened sea-bass.

"There she is!" a man's excited voice cried. "Elena! Elena!"

Tom turned to watch a wild-eyed young man dressed in jeans, paint splashed work boots, and a puffa jacket stride through the smartly-dressed diners and come to a halt at their table.

Face burning, Elena kept her head down.

But even she couldn't ignore the sound of heavy-breathing for ever.

Slowly, she raised her head and stared into the flushed face (yep, he was off his meds) of a man who was slowly becoming her worst nightmare.

Out of the corner of her eye, she spotted the restaurant manager and general manager, Alexander Ludlow, watching the scene.

Crap.

"What are you doing here, David?"

David dropped to his knees with a thud, his eyes beseeching her.

Hell, no.

"I love you, Elena. You know I adore you. You know I'll do anything if you would please, please take me back."

The whole room had gone utterly silent.

Tom spluttered something incomprehensible.

Elena ignored Tom.

She turned in her seat to face David.

"Have you taken your medication today, David?" she asked in a soft voice.

The confused flutter of his eyes confirmed it, no he hadn't.

Taking care to move slow and easy, Elena reached for her purse, took out her cell, scrolled down and pressed call.

In the meantime, David had burst into tears and was rocking on his heels.

"Hey, Charlotte. One of your patients is missing? Yep. He's here at The Hall." Elena listened to the senior nurse of the local psychiatric twenty-four hour care unit issue instructions. "In the restaurant. We'll do our best to keep him calm. Yep."

Alexander Ludlow was making his way towards them. Elena caught his eye and shook her head. He nodded and took a seat at an empty table and whipped out his cell phone.

Elena studied the very sick young man staring up at her as if she was his world.

And her heart broke for him.

"David?"

David stared adoringly at Elena.

"Yes, my darling?"

"Would you like to have a seat? Maybe have a lemonade?"

His eyes glittered strangely and Elena prayed that the hospital team put their foot down.

"I'm not a child, Elena," he said in a totally different voice as his personality morphed from a sobbing adolescent into a dominant adult male. Elena felt the room grow warm. Fear unfurled in her belly. David stood, hands fisted at his side. And she noticed there was no love for her in those strange eyes now. The poor man was, literally, foaming at the mouth. "I'm an adult. I'll join you in a glass of wine."

"You most certainly will not," Tom said, utterly oblivious to Elena's sharp kick under the table.

David whipped around to face Tom.

"Who are you?"

"I'm Elena's boyfriend," Tom said, conveniently forgetting he'd just dumped her.

Now David was breathing heavily through his nose as he very slowly turned back to Elena and got to his feet. There was more than madness in those eyes now and Elena's heart kicked.

AN AFFAIR TO REMEMBER

Oh God.

"Did you give him a blow job, Elena?" David asked. His hand went for the button of his jeans and slid down the zip. "Give me a blow job."

Tom opened his mouth, caught the blistering look Elena sent him and snapped it shut.

Out of the corner of her eye Elena saw Alexander Ludlow and Marc Atelier now approaching David from behind.

David whipped out a very limp dick.

A woman shrieked.

Could this night get any worse?

Elena soon discovered that, yes, it could get worse.

A lot worse.

Now David's groin was in her face.

"Suck it."

Two seconds later David dropped like a stone to the plush carpet.

Marc quickly tucked David's flaccid manhood away and zipped up his jeans.

Torn between relief for herself and anxiety for the man on the floor, she turned to Marc.

"What did you do to him?"

Deep blue eyes stared straight into hers.

Her whole body tingled in a way that made her blink.

"Old ninja trick. Two fingers to pressure points behind the ear. He'll be fine." Marc turned his head to watch four men in white coats arriving. "And here comes the cavalry, too late as usual."

Elena held her head in her hands and breathed through her nose in a world that had gone a little grey round the edges. This was the third time in as many months that David had managed to get out of a secure unit. She'd crossed David's path six months ago as part of the volunteer out-reach team who assisted mental health experts working in the community.

Now she felt a heavy hand on her shoulder.

And she knew without looking up who that hand belonged to, Marc Atelier.

The scent of his cologne spun around her, all lovely and woodsy and her still racing heart did a weird thumpity-thump.

The hand squeezed.

"Hey, are you okay?"

"I'm fine," she said, mortified that she'd unwittingly caused a scene in one of the top restaurants in the county.

"It's my fault she's upset," Tom said. "We broke up tonight."

Elena closed her eyes.

And thank you very much, Tom.

For the first time in Elena's life she wanted to smack the face of a man who wasn't one of her six brothers.

Marc cleared his throat.

Most women who worked at Ludlow Hall and had working ovaries, had the hots for Marc Atelier. Elena was no exception, and no wonder.

He was one of those men that saying he was good-looking just didn't cut it because Marc was tall, a really tall, six foot four or five. Elena knew this because she was five ten herself and her father and brothers were all over six foot. If a miracle happened and she and Marc went on a date, the guy was the perfect height for her, she could even wear heels. Woo hoo! Now Marc simply stared at her with a bemused look in those deep blue eyes. His hair was dark brown, with reddish highlights, and beautifully cut. His face had the bone structure of a Roman Centurion. Yep, Marc Atelier was drop-your-panties-girls gorgeous.

"You're sure you're okay?" Marc asked her.

Elena looked up, met his eyes and noticed his gaze had now moved across the table to her date, with an expression in his eyes that let Tom know Mr. Atelier was less than impressed.

How embarrassing was this?

The heat of mortification prickled up Elena's neck, into her cheeks.

"I'm fine," she said in a cheery voice. "Thanks, Marc."

16

AN AFFAIR TO REMEMBER

He turned to study her face for an unremitting moment, before nodding and walking away.

Why couldn't a real man like Marc ask her out on a date?

He was so tall, so gorgeous and so... capable.

Elena sighed into her napkin, ignoring the prickling behind her eyes and heroically blew her nose. A man like Marc was way, like in a galaxy far far away, out of her league.

"Who the hell is he?" Tom asked, as if he had the right, after *dumping* her, to query her.

Elena was asking herself why she'd let her brother Liam set her up with Tom in the first place?

"He's head of Ferranti Security."

Tom made a face.

"I thought he looked like a goon."

Goon?

Outrage on Marc's behalf rose in her gut.

He might be over six foot four, well built and look like a man who could take care of himself in a tricky situation, but the last thing she'd ever call Marc was a goon.

Elena just looked at the supercilious little man sitting opposite her and wondered what on earth she'd seen in him. If anyone should be doing the dumping tonight it should have been her.

"Didn't you notice that David was ill and not in his right mind, Tom? Don't the police give you basic training in how to deal with people who are, through no fault of their own, unstable?"

Tom blushed.

It was not a good look on him. It made his pale skin blotch.

"I'm in human resources, Elena. I'm not on the front line like Liam. How do you know a crazy person anyway?"

Elena simply stared hard at him in a way that made him blink and shuffle around in his chair.

"I'm a volunteer assistant to the community out-reach team specialising in mental health to help people re-integrate back into society. I was one of the support team allocated to David. When he's on his meds, he's a very nice man."

"I'm surprised your father and brothers are happy to let you do such dangerous work."

Because he'd unerringly hit a sore spot, Elena's chin rose.

"I don't consider it dangerous. What I do in my spare time is my business, Tom."

The frosty tone her voice, Elena realised, was absolutely wasted on him.

He ignored her empty glass, poured himself another glass of Chianti.

"I thought you were upset we broke up," he said.

"Well, I am upset to be dumped in the hotel where I work, thank you for that by the way, Tom, two weeks before Christmas," Elena said in a sharp voice, recovering her fighting spirit fast.

"Here we go," Tom muttered under his breath. He took a sip of wine and spoke to a point above Elena's head, "I just knew you'd be the type of pitiful woman who likes to make a scene when a man changes his mind."

Make a scene?

It was no secret in the Kennedy clan that, when pushed, Elena Margaret Mary had a hair-trigger temper. A genetic strain of temper descended from a long line of hard drinking, hard fighting, Scottish and Irish warriors.

It cost her but Elena managed to rise above the misogynistic little dig, to send him a glittering but very dangerous smile.

"Before you pay the bill and leave, Tom," she said. "I'm somewhat bewildered by the no sex comment."

Tom's face was a picture of sincere bafflement.

She frowned.

"I respect your sacred promise," Tom said.

"What promise is that, Tom?"

"The promise you made to Jesus."

When Elena simply gave him a blank look, Tom rolled his eyes.

"No sex before marriage."

Chapter Three

Elena felt like she'd been whacked on the head by an iron mallet.

She knew her jaw was on the floor.

Her eyes filled.

"Who on earth told you that?" she asked even though in her heart of hearts, she knew the answer.

What she wanted from Tom was verbal confirmation.

"Liam," Tom said. Then he went too pale. "For God's sake don't tell him I told you, Elena."

Liam Kennedy was built like an armoured SUV and was six foot five inches tall. Tom wouldn't come out of a scuffle with her brother in one piece, so Elena simply nodded.

Then she wondered why the hell she was so upset to have a niggling suspicion confirmed. After all, her brothers, especially Liam, had put the men she'd dated under pressure for years.

Years.

She'd either dated men she'd known as boys from school, or friends of her brothers. For years she'd wondered why those men had treated her like nothing more than a good pal. For years she'd wondered what was wrong with her that those men had done nothing more than kiss her good night or tentatively hold her hand.

And right there Elena Kennedy promised to kill her big brother Liam.

Kill him.

It was her heavy cross to bear that Elena was the youngest of seven siblings. Her brothers ranged in age from thirty-seven right through to twenty-eight. Elena herself had been a long awaited daughter after six lively boys. A daughter whose birth had killed her mother (something for which Elena would forever carry the heavy burden of guilt). She'd been brought up in a male dominated household under the too watchful eye of her retired police sergeant father, two brothers who were policemen, one who was an E.R. doctor, and three in the military, one of whom was a Special Forces commander.

Yes, the Kennedy's firmly believed in three things.

God.

And to serve their community and their country.

Actually there were four things.

The fourth was to make sure that at twenty-six Elena Margaret Mary Kennedy remained the oldest virgin in town.

Of course Elena wasn't a virgin, anything but.

However, she was perfectly happy to let her family live under collective mass delusion.

She'd had to be smart about having sex, sneaky even.

It had been great deal easier to be sneaky about sex when she'd attended Manchester University, three hundred miles away from the watchful eyes of her family. Not that she was a slapper or anything like that. Elena Kennedy might have a very healthy libido, but she was... choosy.

Except for Tom, her standards had dropped a bit with him.

Looking at him now, Elena supposed Tom was nice enough, but he certainly hadn't lit much of a hormonal spark. Now she mulled over the reasons why she'd been prepared to sleep with him? Probably because it had been a while since she'd had any... intimacy.

Her work, ruling the reception team with a fluffy duster, at Ludlow Hall kept her pretty busy. And now she'd been promoted, she lived on site in one of the beautifully fitted out old coach houses, work had taken over her life. Not that that was a problem, because Elena adored her job. Adored working for the gorgeous Nico Ferranti and Alexander Ludlow. She adored Nico and Alexander's wives, their children and the whole family vibe that surrounded Ludlow Hall. The problem was that she didn't date staff. She definitely didn't date guests, because if a relationship went wrong things would become very sticky work-wise. And those self-imposed rules meant she'd had very slim pickings over the last year.

AN AFFAIR TO REMEMBER

Now Elena wondered, looking over the table at a very embarrassed Tom, if she'd become simply desperate to have sex, to feel that intimacy, with just anyone?

"Plus, you're not really my type, Elena," Tom was saying now. "You're too..."

The words suddenly snapped her right back into the moment.

Her brows rose.

"Too what, Tom?"

Tom took another swig of his wine, obviously determined to get his money's worth since he was paying for it.

"It's just... I don't find you very... likeable."

Elena's jaw hit the floor yet again.

"You don't *like* me?"

Everybody liked her.

Everybody.

Tom rolled his eyes, and it was the final straw that broke the camel's back.

"You're the first person I've ever met who doesn't like me, Tom. I'm very likeable. Anybody will tell you. Let's ask the waiter." Elena waved over the head waiter who materialised at her side. "Do you like me, Gerard? Tell me the truth."

Gerard was sixty-five, happily married, a father of two, and proud granddaddy of four tearaways under the age of nine.

Now Gerard's poached-egg eyes twinkled into hers as he took her hand in his and pressed his lips to her fingers.

"Elena, sweetheart, I adore you."

Elena turned to a seriously unimpressed Tom and gave him a smile that didn't reach her eyes.

"See?"

"You have a very strange sense of humour," Tom said, not giving an inch. "You find things funny that are not funny. And you're too..." His forehead creased as he feebly struggled to find the right word in his feeble brain. "Rugged."

"Rugged?" she echoed, all at sea.

"I meant, robust. You carried that rabbit hutch all by yourself when I couldn't budge it." Now he frowned. "A man likes to feel like a man around his woman, Elena."

His woman?

"It's not my fault you've no upper body strength, Tom. Maybe if you spent more time lifting weights at the gym and less time lifting a glass in the pub, you'd be able to lift the hutch for *your* rabbit, might I remind you?"

"See? There you go, getting all pissy and mouthy."

"Pissy and..."

She snapped her mouth shut because it suddenly occurred to Elena there was echo in her head. An echo that kept repeating the words spilling from Tom's sulky mouth.

Now Tom's pale grey eyes went sulky, too.

"Yeah, you talk to guys as if you're one of the guys. I like my women soft and warm and sweet and... womanly."

Elena's face burned.

It wasn't the first time, not by a long shot, a man had said she was like one of the guys.

All the guys treated her like one of the guys.

Her eyes filled and she'd rather die a slow and agonising death than show Tom, (who'd morphed right before her very eyes into an evil little gremlin shooting unerringly accurate arrows that stung) how much those words had upset her.

Was it her fault she didn't have a mother or sisters to guide her through life? It was true that she was five foot ten and had what her doting father called, 'big bones'. It was also true she was rubbish at talking like a girly girl or walking like a girly girl or wearing girly girl things. She even wore her hair in short pixie crop because she was rubbish with her hair and doing girly things with it, too.

Elena just looked at Tom knocking back the rest of the wine and wasn't sure she was going to be able to stop her hands gripping his puny little throat and strangling him.

"There you go," Tom said. Taking out his wallet, he carefully counted out six ten pound notes and placed them on the table.

"Should be enough to cover half, after your staff discount. See you around."

He stood.

"Tom?"

"Yeah?"

"I really don't like you very much either."

Tom shook his head before he turned and walked away.

Elena did her level best to ignore the whispers and the stares from other diners as she picked up the wine bottle and realised it was empty.

Little shit.

Chapter Four

In his man-cave, Marc had watched the whole scene in the restaurant between Elena and her date unfold with interest.

At the point where Elena went to pour wine and came up empty, he kept one eye on her as he picked up his cell phone, slid down his contact list and pressed call. At the same time he toggled the car park cameras, watched Elena's *date* stroll to his car. He picked up a pen and made a note of Tom's car registration number.

"Hey, Andy. Who do you have on traffic duty tonight?"

Inspector Andy Bradshaw was the local Chief Inspector of police and a good pal.

The way Marc figured it, as the head of security for the Ferranti Group and based at Ludlow Hall, he had a duty of care to the local community and road users. If an asshole wanted to drink and drive that was the asshole's personal choice, but Marc wasn't going to have an asshole leave the bar at Ludlow Hall and killing or seriously injuring someone on his watch and on his conscience. The fact that it was a timely revenge on the dick who'd abandoned Elena right in the middle of the up-market restaurant at Ludlow Hall, in front of her colleagues, was just the icing on the cake.

"Gotta dark blue Volvo, registration number..." Marc gave the number. "Road's are icy tonight. He's had the best part of a bottle of vintage Chianti. And I have on camera the reception staff offering to phone him a taxi, but he blew them off." He listened to Andy sending a message to traffic cops only too happy to take another asshole off the road.

Andy returned his attention to Marc. "Hear you had an escaped mental patient on your hands this evening. Nico's asking for action, this is the third time David Evans has harassed Elena Kennedy. Nico's worried."

AN AFFAIR TO REMEMBER

"Maybe I should speak to the hospital myself," Marc said. "It appears their security protocols are not up to speed."

"Budget cuts," Andy said. "Gotta go, thanks for the tip-off."

"My pleasure, if I don't see you and Susan and the kids before the big fat man climbs down the chimney, have a good Christmas."

Marc pressed end call, his gaze rose to the restaurant screen. He watched Elena rise from the table, wriggle the hem of her dress down, lift her purse, and stride out of the restaurant and into the bar.

His tongue stroked the inside of his cheek as she slid like melted butter on hot toast onto a high bar stool and wiggled her fingers at the bar manager. As that fine little butt hit the black leather seat, her dress had risen a couple of inches exposing a very nice length of lean and toned thigh. Very nice. Marc checked the time, he had half an hour before his shift ended. Thirty minutes. His eyes narrowed as a good looking guy approached Elena.

The guy leaned on the bar and slid, as far as Marc was concerned, too close to Elena.

Marc's eyes narrowed even further when he saw her smile into the guys face.

Oh no.

Elena'd had a bad night.

She'd had an escaped mental patient hit on her.

Her dork of a boyfriend had dumped her in the worst possible way.

Not that Marc was sorry for that, because it meant that, at last, he could make a play for Elena Kennedy with a clear conscience.

However, the girl was quite understandably upset.

Vulnerable.

Which meant that to make herself feel better, there was a possibility Elena Kennedy might be in a mood to tango with a stranger.

However, the man who was at this moment chatting her up, was no stranger to Marc.

He was a man that Marc knew would be more than happy to tango with Elena.

Not gonna happen.

Not on his watch.

Marc picked up a walkie-talkie from his desk, pressed the button.

"Neil? Can you cover for me until Steve signs in? I'll be in the bar. No, no trouble. Thanks."

Three minutes later there was a single rap on the door and Neil, aka The Hulk, entered.

"Yo, what's up, boss?"

Marc closed his laptop, locked it in the bottom drawer of his desk and turned to his deputy.

"I'm off duty until Monday. Any trouble you know the drill. I'll be in the bar."

He stood.

Neil slipped into his boss's empty chair, leaned back and the chair creaked dangerously.

"No probs. It's looking like a quiet night."

"Let's hope it stays that way."

"From your mouth to God's ear."

Elena Kennedy was a woman in dire need of a very stiff drink.

She wiggled her fingers at Scott, the bar manager and he moved to serve her.

"Hey gorgeous. What's your poison? A Pinot Grigio?" Scott mentioned her favourite tipple, polished the shiny bar with a soft white cloth and smiled into her face. Scott was not only a good-looking guy with a heart of solid gold, he was happily married with a baby daughter. Why was it all the good ones were taken?

"Nope, I need something a helluva lot stronger," she said in a tone that meant business and caused Scott's brow to rise.

"You don't have a head for the hard stuff," Scott reminded her.

Scott knew this because he'd known Elena since she was five.

Right there, Elena fumed, was the downside of living in the same small town all her life.

AN AFFAIR TO REMEMBER

A strong shoulder nudged hers and a waft of very expensive cologne made her take a deep breath. Very nice. Elena turned to find a stranger checking her out with something like admiration, and was that attraction in his dark eyes?

Oh yes, it was.

And was that a tingle in the region of her ovaries?

Yes, there was a definite buzz low in her pelvis.

Elena found herself smiling.

And Hello, Mr. Tall (very tall. Woo Hoo!) Dark And Handsome.

"Bad day?" Mr. TDH asked.

Elena did a quick mental scan of the stranger.

Nice voice, too, deep and masculine.

Sharp suit.

Expensive tie.

White teeth.

Strong jaw.

A Kirk Douglas dimple in his smooth chin.

Nice.

"Do you count being flashed by an escaped mental patient and being dumped by your boyfriend a bad day?" she said, telling him the truth and nothing but the truth.

Dark eyes danced merrily into hers, and she realised he thought she was kidding.

If only.

Her battered and bruised ego perked right up.

"What you need," he said. "Is an After Shock."

Elena didn't have the first clue what he was talking about, but she took a wild guess.

She smiled.

"Are you offering to buy me a drink?"

For the first time in her life Elena Kennedy was openly flirting and she liked it.

She liked it an awful lot.

Now Mr. TDH smiled right back at her as he turned his very fit body into hers.

27

And her tingles had tingles.

"I'd be delighted to buy you a drink." He held out his hand. "Odin Jensen."

He had long fingers, nice nails and his hand felt smooth and cool.

He had a strong grip.

Nice.

"Elena Kennedy, lovely to meet you." She turned to Scott, who'd been watching the exchange with wary eyes. "I'll have an After Shock, trust me, I need it."

"Are you sure, Elena? It'll blow your head off."

Elena knew Scott was besties with two of her brothers and could feel her siblings' overprotective influence in the tone of his voice and in the way that Scott was looking at her with watchful eyes.

Well, fuck that.

She wanted a drink and by god she was going to have one.

"I'm not driving. Just serve me the drink, Scottie. In fact, make it a double."

The nickname from childhood did the trick, the bar manager looked at her for two beats too long before he turned a very polite face to her benefactor.

"And what can I get you, sir?"

"Glenmorangie Signet, a double please and put the drinks on my tab."

Elena's eyes went huge when a shot glass was placed in front of her, Scott struck a match and set her drink on fire.

Bloody hell.

When the flames died down, she simply stared at the glass without a clue what to do next.

"You down it in one," Odin whispered in her ear.

Scott was staring at her, his eyes just *daring* her to drink it.

Elena's chin jerked in a reckless way that had her companion laugh softly.

She lifted the glass and turned to the lovely Odin and gave him the benefit of her best eyelash flutter.

What was the worst thing that could happen to her?

She'd already had the night from hell.

They clinked glasses.

"Cheers," Elena said, throwing caution to the wind and knocked it back in one.

The glass fisted in her hands, she could feel blood leaking from her brain as heat set her throat alight and burned a searing path down to her belly.

Ooooh boy.

Her eyes watered.

Her nose watered.

"Breathe," Odin suggested, obviously enjoying himself.

"That was a single," Scott informed her in a silky I-told-you-so voice. He leaned on the bar and right into her face. "Sure you can manage a double?"

Pig.

Now, in the normal course of events, Elena Kennedy was not a stupid person.

In her professional life, she was renowned for keeping a cool head in a crisis, good judgement and a healthy dose of common sense. If she had a single weakness it was stubbornness. And Elena knew she was being stubborn now. After the night she'd had there was no way she was going to back down.

Plus, she was feeling absolutely fabulous, *dahling*!

Euphoric.

The scenes with David and then Tom, felt like no big deal.

No big deal at all, baby.

"Gimme me a double," she said with a bravado and a glitter in her eyes that would have made her brothers run for the hills.

She didn't see Odin shake his head at Scott and mouth *'Single'*.

While Scott poured her drink, she didn't notice her dress creep up another couple of inches either as she turned to her new companion, who was fast becoming her bestest friend in the whole wide world.

She grinned up into his gorgeously gorgeous face.

"So, Odin Jensen. Isn't Odin the name of a Viking God and father of the great and glorious Thor with the Big Hammer? And didn't Odin have one eye?"

Odin laughed, and at the same time slipped a glass of water into her hand.

"Drink this. It's good for shock, too."

Elena did as she was told.

The water tasted delicious.

Strangely enough she was feeling a little... hot, all of a sudden.

Now Odin slid his arm around her waist and Elena leaned into him companionably. He smelled fab so she took another sniff, this time of his neck. Her eyes dropped to his mouth. A wonderful mouth, she decided. Kissable.

Odin waited until she'd drained the glass of water to respond.

"Well done, not many people know that Odin is, indeed, a Viking god. He's also the god of ecstasy. He makes people do things they don't normally do."

"Naughty things?" she whispered, and licked her lips.

Who was this woman? A voice in her head demanded to know.

Elena had no idea, but she just *loved* the new woman who'd taken over her mind, her body.

Her eyes met Odin's and saw that they were laughing, in a good way, in a nice way.

"Baby, I'm the god of ecstasy, what do you think?"

Scott cleared his throat, loudly, and placed another shot glass in front of her then set it alight.

"Elena, honey. I don't think this is a good idea," Scott warned her.

His warning fell on deaf ears.

Elena stared at him, gave Scott slitty eyes, a pouty mouth.

And managed to stop herself, just in time, to give him two fingers, because that would most definitely be something that a *guy* would do to another guy.

Not ladylike behaviour at all.

Oh no, tonight she was going to be all woman.

Then Elena lifted her shot glass and knocked it back.

Her fist punched her chest once, twice.

AN AFFAIR TO REMEMBER

She was, *woman, hear her roooaaar!*

Scott turned his head to look toward the entrance to the bar and was that relief in his eyes?

"Thank you, Jesus," Scott said.

Chapter Five

Elena turned her head to see who had Scott all excited, but the room spun and Odin's arm tightened around her waist.

"Evening, O," Marc said as he grabbed Elena around the waist and hauled her off the stool. For some reason the muscles in her legs were confused because they wobbled and went all noodly. "Thanks for looking after my girl. She's had a bad day."

Because she was just loving the way a big strong man was holding her, Elena missed the way two alpha males eyed each other over her head, missed the way Odin nodded once, lifted his glass to Marc and settled himself into Elena's empty stool.

"Take good care of her," Odin told Marc. "She's a special lady."

For some reason Elena didn't mind being dragged away from the god Odin, she raised her hand in the air, wiggled her fingers.

"Bye, bye, god of ecstasy. Thank you so much for the After Shock."

"God of ecstasy?" a voice said in her ear.

She blinked up into Marc's face, saw him run his tongue inside his cheek.

If she thought Odin smelled amazeballs, it was nothing, nothing, compared to the *deeelicious* scent of Marc Atelier. His strong arm held her close as he supported her to the cloakroom and checked out her coat. As he helped her into a warm coat of the finest cashmere and buttoned it right up to the neck, Elena just let her body fall into his.

She buried her nose in his neck and took a deep inhale.

"You smell amazing. You always smell amazing," she told him and smiled up into his face.

She was bombed.

Marc checked her hazel eyes.

Yep.

Bombed.

He bit his lip as he read adoration and lust for him in those big hazel eyes.

She looked wild, wicked and wanton.

She looked like a woman who needed very badly to get laid.

Marc wasn't stupid enough to take it personally, since she'd looked at Odin in exactly the same way. His ego took a little knock, but Marc told himself to get over it.

His shaft jerked, reminding him that he'd had a constant hard-on all night since he'd seen her walk into the restaurant in that dress.

It was a damn shame Elena wasn't sober or he'd be acting on that need.

Marc hadn't been with a woman, hadn't wanted a woman, since his father had passed.

Now he settled Elena in a chair with her purse on her lap. He pulled on his coat and prepared to trudge up the well-lit path, a five minute walk, from Ludlow Hall to Elena's coach house. There was no point in calling a taxi. And he couldn't drive her there because he'd left his car at home, a house situated less than a hundred yards from hers.

Elena didn't resist when he took her small purse, opened it and found her door keys.

Marc stuffed her purse in his coat pocket.

The walk would probably do her good.

He hoped.

Outside, he knew the temperature had dropped like a stone, so he wound his cashmere scarf around her neck and hefted her to her feet.

"Let's go."

His arm wound around her waist and her arm wound around his.

The crazy giggle that came from her throat was yet another reminder that she was absolutely wasted.

The Elena Kennedy he knew, the one who manned reception, had never giggled in her life.

As they left the warmth of the hotel and hit the path Elena took a deep breath and then another.

Her feet in her high heels stumbled and Marc steadied her.

"You okay?" He bent his knees to look into her face.

Her hand went to her head.

"'kay," she said. "My head's spinning."

His arm went around her waist again as they moved forward.

"Yeah, well a couple of After Shocks on top of wine will do that."

"I don't have a head for alcohol."

"You don't say," he said.

"Yep. I'm rubbish at drinking competitions, too." She went quiet for a moment. "Marc?"

"Elena?"

She sniffed.

"Do you see me as just one of the guys?"

He stopped dead, bent his knees again to look at her face to see if she was yanking his chain.

And saw with something like shock that Elena was deadly serious.

Big brown eyes were filled with what looked like hurt, looked like confusion, as they stared into his.

No way could he lie.

"Baby, I regard you as one hell of a sexy woman."

Her eyes filled.

Oh shit.

Marc Atelier might be a tough guy, but female tears terrified him.

Elena gave him a pitiful attempt at a smile.

"Thank you so much for saying that, Marc. You're a very nice man. That was a very nice thing to say," she said, as if he was spinning her a line and she didn't believe a single word.

He shook his head in dismay.

He was a *very nice* man, was he?

She couldn't be more wrong.

Marc Atelier didn't have a *nice* bone in his body.

AN AFFAIR TO REMEMBER

As soon as Miss. Elena Kennedy was sober, they'd be having a very long talk.

By the time they arrived at her door, she was shivering.

The porch light was lit.

And behind thick curtains, the sitting room light was on, too.

As he held her up with one hand, Marc unlocked a large oak door with the other and shoved her through and into the warmth.

It didn't escape his attention that Elena hadn't engaged the security alarm.

Marc frowned.

He'd be having a little chat about that, too.

A woman living alone couldn't be too careful.

Closing the heavy door behind him, he turned to fiddle with the central heating thermostat to turn it up. Then he opened the oak door into the open plan sitting room/kitchen and settled her into a large comfy chair next to the wood-burner, which burned low in a vast fire-place. Elena was tidy. The place was immaculate. The interior design in the coach houses was impressive. He shrugged off his coat, loosened his tie, as he looked at the cosy and snug seating arrangements. Set around a chunky coffee table, there was a big sofa in crushed velvet the colour of dark chocolate. He dumped his coat on the arm of a chair. The serving table that sat behind the sofa and divided the eating and dining space had two glass lamps with shades matching the curtains placed at each end along with a huge vase of fresh winter flowers with springs of red berries woven through it. There were two fat chairs covered in a tartan check design in russets and creams that went well with thick interlined curtains in silk the colour of old gold at the window and French doors. Marc had seen plenty of Ferranti senior staff quarters around the world and gave this designer ten out ten. Hand crafted wooden shutters kept the heat in at the kitchen window. Six hand thrown terracotta pots on the kitchen window ledge held a variety of herbs. It appeared Elena liked to cook. Although it also appeared Elena didn't go in for girly cushions and candles and dust catchers. However, she'd crammed the heavy oak mantelpiece and every available surface with family photos of her father and brothers, interlaced with sprigs of fresh holly in a nod to the season. The place had a lovely warm and comfortable vibe.

Marc turned his attention to the woman sprawled in the chair, hazel eyes flickering with gold as she stared unseeing into the glowing log burner. He added a couple of logs to keep it going through the night.

"Let's take your coat off," he said in a friendly tone. "Are you still cold?"

She blinked and looked a little surprised to see him.

Her wide smile made him smile, too.

It appeared Elena was a happy drunk and Marc thanked heaven for small mercies.

At some point, she'd kicked off her heels.

Now when she stood, the top of her head came under his chin.

He inhaled the scent of her floral shampoo, warm woman and eau de After Shock.

For the first time since he'd met her, Elena appeared slight and very vulnerable.

As he took her coat, goose bumps rose over her smooth, creamy flesh. And Marc's hands itched to touch, to taste. He tried very hard not to notice how her nipples strained against the fine fabric of her dress. He grabbed her coat, and his, and moved to the tiny hall to hang them on the wall hooks. When he returned to the room Elena was standing in exactly the same spot, swaying on her stocking feet.

With gentle hands, he pushed her down into the chair.

"Why don't you sit down, sweetheart." He wrapped a handy woollen throw around her for warmth, to hide all that skin and to stop the whisper of temptation in his ear. "And I'll get you a hot drink. What would you like?"

Eyes filled with nothing but love and affection for him met his.

Common sense told him she was sloshed, not to take any notice of how she looked at him or what she said, but something clicked in the region of Marc's carefully guarded heart.

AN AFFAIR TO REMEMBER

He cleared his throat.

"Are you hungry? Fancy a sandwich?"

Fancy me?

She shook her head.

"Tea would be nice."

Elena had a wide and sensitive mouth that just begged to be kissed.

His shaft went rock hard.

He'd kiss her tomorrow, Marc promised himself fiercely.

The cupboards and appliances in the kitchens of the coach houses, all six of them, were organised in exactly the same way, which made doing the inventory check-list for breakages etc., before and after a person moved in, easy to maintain.

Marc switched on the stainless steel kettle, grabbed a couple of mugs, noting that she'd replaced the standard issue white with her own. They were large and the colour of ivory with tiny lilac flowers. Girly. He grinned. Her teapot matched the mugs and he warmed it with boiling water before placing two teabags in the pot and adding boiled water. He placed the mugs, a jug of milk and sugar and teapot on the tray and moved into the sitting room. Without asking her, he poured the tea, added three teaspoons of sugar and milk to the mug and handed it to her. After pouring tea for himself, Marc settled down to watch the myriad of expressions crossing her beautiful face.

She was staring and smiling into the fire and Marc wondered what she was thinking.

He didn't have to wonder long.

"Marc, since the very first moment I saw you walk into Ludlow Hall," Elena said in a dreamy voice as she stared into the fire. "You made my lady bits tingle."

Chapter Six

Happily existing in a blissful and contented place, Elena watched Marc inhale his tea and struggle not to spill it as he coughed up a lung.

Calmly, she handed him a couple of tissues plucked from the box on the coffee table.

"Christ," he said, as he mopped his streaming eyes.

Somewhere, fluttering on the extreme edges of a mind living in a happy haze of alcohol, somewhere where common sense lived, Elena knew that how she felt in this moment, in that wondrous sense of *rightness*, that this strange new world she was living in, was in fact, all wrong.

And she couldn't give a hot damn.

She waited until his eyes claimed hers.

"I dream about you all the time," she said with brutal honesty.

The poor man shook his head, his blue eyes wide and sincere.

"Elena, sweetheart. I don't think you should be telling me this. It's not you speaking, it's After Shock. And it's named that for a reason."

Aww, poor baby, he was worried she'd embarrass herself?

What a *nice* guy.

Well, Elena couldn't care less.

For some strange reason it was really important, crucial even, for her to tell him how she felt.

So she leaned over to pat the hand that was resting on the arm of the sofa.

She studied that hand now.

The man had lovely hands with long fingers and short, clean nails.

From his wrist, he also had a sprinkling of fine dark hair peeping out of the cuff of his white cotton shirt.

AN AFFAIR TO REMEMBER

She wondered if he had a snake of dark hair leading to the impressive bulge between his legs, too. Her eyes rested on that bulge as the tingling between her legs clicked up a notch.

"I love After Shocks. And let me tell you something else," she said.

Her eyes slid up his body to his face.

His Adam's apple bobbed twice.

"What's that?" he asked in a hoarse voice.

She blinked into his eyes.

"In my dreams you and I are in this very room. My panties are at my ankles, you bend me over the arm of the sofa and take me hard and fast until I scream. Do you think you could do that, Marc?"

Yes.

His dick was screaming that it could most definitely do that.

Right *now* in fact.

If only she wasn't pissed and didn't have a clue what she was saying.

Jeeeeeezus.

It appeared a couple of After Shock's were better than truth serum.

Unable to listen to another word, Marc leapt to his feet.

"Okay, that's enough. Drink up your tea like a good girl and we'll get you up to bed."

"I've finished my tea. Are we going to bed to fuck?"

It cost him, but Marc ignored the question as he whipped the mug out of her hand and placed it on the tea tray.

It terrified him that his hand was shaking.

As he moved around the coffee table to take a hold of her slim wrist, Marc found his arms full of a very warm and very willing woman. Her arms were around his neck, those wonderful breasts now plastered against his chest and her pelvis slid against his in a way that made him grit his teeth and just hang on. No matter how hard he tried, his dick went so hard he closed his eyes.

"Oh my. You *are* happy to see me, big boy."

Oh God, baby Jesus, Christ help him.

He trembled.

She laughed.

A throaty, sultry sound that made him groan out loud.

When her hand slid down his front to rest on his throbbing shaft and squeeze, his eyes rolled back in his head.

Marc hadn't lived thirty-four years without women touching him like this. Of course they had. But he'd never, ever, experienced the force of nature that was Elena Kennedy. Her touch, the purr in her throat, the way she smelled, did something to him that was beyond pleasure, beyond pain.

If only she was sober.

If only she was in her right mind.

But she wasn't, he reminded himself desperately.

He was a good man.

And good men did not take advantage of a woman under the influence, no matter what she said, no matter what she did and no matter what his dick demanded.

She was licking his neck now, still rubbing herself up and down his body like a cat in heat. This needed to end, right now.

Without a word, he scooped her up in his arms, marched through the door, up the narrow stairs (not without difficulty) and through a process of elimination found her bedroom.

Her little yelp of delight when he tossed her on the bed seriously tested his resolve.

Annoyance with her, and with himself, was beginning to churn and burn hot and bright in his gut now. And that annoyance was winning the battle with a brutal arousal.

Without a lick of conscience, he started to rummage through a beautiful antique set of drawers. Her silk underwear was predominately in neutral colours, expensive and incredibly feminine with lace and ribbons. The thought of her wearing the sheer bras, the panties, under her crisp and tailored uniform every day, nearly made him come in his pants.

"Ooooh Maaaarc," the siren sang his name in a way that made him close eyes.

Not a religious man, Marc prayed.

And he promised himself that tomorrow he'd make her pay for this.

He slammed the drawer shut and opened the next to find a pair of white flannel pyjama bottoms with pink teddy bears. Perfect. Because he knew there was no way in hell he'd have coped with something in silk or lace. It would have fucking killed him. He grabbed the flannel pyjama bottoms as a man might grab a life belt in a stormy sea. In the next drawer, he found an oversized pink T-shirt. Even better, so he grabbed that, too, and turned around.

And stopped dead, his heart thudding like a pneumatic drill against his ribs.

He broke out in a cold sweat.

Oh. My. God.

One long leg was stretched up to the ceiling, her toe pointed like a ballet dancer as she tossed the black hold up silk stocking to the floor. Slowly, so slowly, she brought the leg down. The woman had fabulous stomach muscles. She bent the other leg as her hands slid up, up her thigh, to slide off the other stocking. She turned her head to watch his face and licked her lips. When she tossed the stocking towards him, he couldn't look away. Then she pulled the hem of her dress up to her waist, wiggled down the bed and placed her thumbs either side of tiny panties of sheer black silk. The Brazilian between her thighs made him blink as both legs were bent at the knees, as she pulled down her panties exposing the swollen pink lips of her sex. In a smooth move, she whipped off her panties before stretching both legs to the ceiling and pointing her toes.

And Marc knew that if he didn't get out of there, right now, he'd do something that would shame him as a man and make her hate him for ever.

He moved fast and flipped her over onto her belly.

Unfortunately, the move made her think they were going to do something kinky because she was on her knees with her bare ass in the air.

His hand itched, really itched, to spank that tight little bottom.

He actually closed his eyes and visualised the scene.

But that could wait for another day.

Clenching his jaw so hard he was lucky not to shatter his molars, he pulled her legs down and quickly dressed her in her teddy bear pyjama bottoms. He should have felt better. But as he turned her over and whipped her dress over her head and arms, her magnificent breasts were released. Gorgeous, was all he could think. But although Marc whimpered, he battled on and the way bitter disappointment filled those big hazel eyes and made them swim made him feel like a complete bastard. However, he ruthlessly ignored those big eyes as he tugged her pink T-shirt over her head. His hands were shaking as he tucked the thick comforter around her.

By this time his dick was howling between his legs, but Marc soldiered on.

He marched into her en-suite and filled a large glass with cold water from the tap.

By a process of elimination, he rummaged through feminine unmentionables in cupboards and drawers to find aspirin for the headache from hell she would surely have in the morning. He popped two from the packet before stalking back into her bedroom.

Her eyes were teary and drowsy as she sat up and took the pills and swallowed the water like a good little girl.

"I'll leave the bathroom light on in case you get up in the night. How are you feeling?" he asked in a tight voice.

Heat rose up her neck and into her cheeks.

And he was delighted to see it.

Her eyes were a little clearer, too.

"Fine. Thank you for looking after me," she said, and her chin wobbled. When her bottom lip trembled, he felt like crying himself. "I'm sorry you don't want to fuck me."

Ooooookay.

So the After Shocks had still not quite worn off.

He placed her cell on the bedside table.

"If you feel unwell, give me a call. My number's at the top of the list, on speed dial. I'm just up the path. Don't hesitate to call me."

AN AFFAIR TO REMEMBER

He really should stay the night, but there was no way in hell he could be under the same roof and not take her. If Elena was throwing up then he'd definitely stay, but her eyes looked clearer and she didn't look grey and pasty. If anything she looked amazing, all rosy and glowing.

She sniffed pathetically as she settled into her pillows, tugged the comforter right up to her chin.

Lord, she was so beautiful, even if she did look pitiful.

It shouldn't have made his throat ache.

It shouldn't have made his eyes sting.

His balls were actually throbbing in time to the hectic beat of his heart.

And right there Marc made a firm pledge to the universe, to karma, to any deity or divine being who might be listening that Elena Kennedy was going to live to regret putting him through hell this night.

Chapter Seven

Elena awoke precisely ten hours after the moment she'd shut her eyes.

Her curtains were closed, but light bathed her big bed from her en-suite bathroom.

Her throat was a little dry and she had a strange taste in her mouth, but her head was clear. Rolling onto her back, Elena stared at the ceiling and tried to remember the events of the night before.

As if she was watching a movie, various scenes flickered through her mind. She dimly recalled some sort of kerfuffle with poor David. Then she remembered the buzzing in her ears and the hectic beat of her heart she'd had during the experience with David and the fact that her boyfriend Tom had dumped her. Now that Tom was no longer part of her life, Elena reckoned she should at least have felt little pang of... something. But she didn't, except that she wished she'd dumped Tom first. A natural reaction, she told herself. Then she remembered a Viking god, Odin. Oh yeah, a lovely drop-dead-gorgeous tall, dark and handsome guy. She wondered what had happened to him? Then her brow wrinkled when she remembered Scott telling not to drink something, what was it again? Oh yeah, After Shock.

Elena tended to stick to a single glass of white wine or a lite beer or soft drinks when she partied. A particularly bad experience at Uni had put her off hard liquor, she didn't have the head for it.

As she wrinkled her brow, she remembered tossing back the shot, the burn in her throat, scorching a path down her digestive tract to pool in her belly, to spread through her system. The potent liquor had brought a tear to her eye. However, it was the 'after' affect that really stood out. She'd felt absolutely wonderful. Up for anything. Ready to take on the world and everyone in it. Especially sex!

However, other memories, unrelenting, now fast forwarded her memory.

Marc Atelier taking charge of poor David at the table in the restaurant, while a beyond stupid Tom simply sat and watched the action with his mouth hanging open. Then later, much later, Marc putting his arm around her, putting on her coat, winding his scarf around her neck. The freezing cold as they'd walked home, together. Marc opening her door. Marc in her sitting room, making her sweet tea. The sort of tea her daddy made her when she'd been little and was sick. And Marc ensuring she drank the tea.

Then Elena shot up in bed, her skin suddenly clammy, as her eyes went wide with something like utter horror as she remembered quite distinctly that she'd asked Marc to... to... *fuck* her?

All she could hear was the sound of her heart thundering in her ears.

The room spun.

And she'd touched him down... *there!*

He'd been so hard, so big, so terribly aroused.

Now she remembered how he'd groaned, how he'd begged her to stop.

She could smell him, taste him, hear him.

Omigod.

Unable to sit still a moment longer, Elena leapt out of bed and dragged open her curtains to find it snowing heavily beneath a leaden sky.

But she couldn't see it because her mind was merciless as it poured memories on top of memories along with feelings of lust, of need, of desire, of secrets told that should *never*, ever be told.

Dear god, had she really said those things to his face about her secret dreams, about him bending her over the sofa?

Had she *really* knelt on her bed and offered him her bare bottom?

Closing her eyes she shivered in reaction, torn between arousal and dismay and could feel the way his hands had trembled as he'd handled her as he'd stripped her dress, as he'd dressed her in her pyjamas, as he'd fought not to touch her.

What on earth had she done?

How could she look the man in the eye again?

How could she face him at work?

Elena whimpered, pressed her fingers to her mouth.

Now she really did feel sick.

But her heart wouldn't stop racing as she spun to look at her bed, to see the evidence of what she'd done. The way she'd stripped like a hooker. The stockings were on the floor, along with her panties, *proof*, and her dress. And now she stared down at her pyjama bottoms. The ones her best friend Lucy had bought her as a joke. Pink teddy bears and a huge pink T-shirt.

Omigod.

Now she raced into her bathroom to find a box of aspirin opened on the sink unit.

He'd given her two little pills and told her drink all the water in the glass.

And she'd done it.

Panic gripped her lungs and squeezed hard.

She stripped off her pyjamas, tossed them in the laundry basket and stepped into the shower.

The first sting of water was so icy she cried out loud.

Served her right, the voice of reason spoke.

As the water warmed, grew hot, she adjusted the thermostat.

And went through the motions of shampooing, conditioning, rinsing her hair. Then she slathered a foaming gel all over her body, avoiding her tingling nipples and the ache low in her belly. Even though mortification held her firmly in its grip, even though she'd no idea how she would ever look Marc in the eye again, she was incredibly aroused.

Now Elena recalled his face, his eyes, as he'd looked at her.

Maybe she'd imagined desire?

Maybe she'd imagined lust?

Maybe she'd imagined a mix of frustration and annoyance?

Maybe she needed her head examined?

Head spinning with too many hectic thoughts, she wrapped her hair in a warm towel, grabbed a large bath sheet, wound it around her body as she wandered into her bedroom and sank to the stool in front of her dressing table. She studied her face in the mirror and saw it all. Her eyes were too big for her face. She was too pale. And she was trembling with reaction.

How on earth could a dinner date with Tom have turned into this?

Her whole body was wound too tight, but she went through the motions of moisturising her face, of blow drying her short hair, of applying a little colour to her lips, her cheeks. God knew she needed it. It didn't take long. Like an automaton, she moved to her closet, dragged out ancient yoga pants, black, and an oversized sweatshirt, black, that had belonged to one of her brothers. In spite of the central heating her feet were freezing, so she pulled on thick socks and shoved her feet into ankle boots made of soft sheepskin, black.

Her eye was drawn to her cell phone on the small table at the side of her bed.

Elena bit her lip as she moved to pick it up, checked the number at the top and sure enough there was Marc's number.

Sinking to the edge of the bed, she wondered what to do for the best.

Should she phone him?

Maybe thank him for looking after her?

Maybe thank him for not taking advantage of her?

Elena tossed the phone on her unmade bed and held her spinning head in her hands as all the things, the words she'd used, spun into her mind again and again.

Eventually, Elena knew she had to get on with the day, eat breakfast, tidy the house, and then she'd decide what to do. She'd achieve nothing by sitting in her bedroom worried sick like a lemming.

With the phone clutched in her hand, Elena wandered down stairs, noticed her coat hanging on the peg in the hall, remembered Marc had hung it there. As soon as she entered her sitting room, the evidence of the night before was all there, too. The tray with tea things. The wood burner was still glowing. It needed wood, so she fed it and then turned to open her sitting room curtains to a day as grey as her mood. And felt a lot better once the cold light of day entered the room.

She picked up the tray, moved into the kitchen.

Then she opened the shutters, let in a skinny wintry light and smiled when she spotted a couple of robins playing tag as they fed from the selection of nuts and seeds in her bird feeder. As if walking in a dream, she switched on the kettle, popped a couple of slices of wholemeal toast into the toaster, rummaged around the fridge for cheese to add to the toast and milk for coffee. She'd just poured herself a mug of strong java and was standing leaning back against the smooth wood of her counter top, staring into space, when there was a brisk knock at the door.

And right away her heart took a mighty leap right into her mouth.

The thought spun into her chaotic mind that maybe she should ignore the door, pretend she was out, or still asleep. Maybe it wasn't Marc. Then Elena bit her lip, she hadn't heard the sound of a car engine. No sane person would be out driving in this weather. But Marc only lived a short distance away so he'd probably walked. Again there was a knock at the door, and this time it sounded impatient.

Taking a deep breath, Elena moved to place the mug on the counter top and realised her hands were shaking. But she straightened her spine and moved through her sitting room into the hall.

As the old song said, it was time to face the music.

Elena opened the door.

48

Chapter Eight

Marc knew as soon as he saw her pale face and the way her shoulders hunched as if ready for a blow that Elena remembered the night before. She was bound to have regrets because she'd no idea that he wanted her just as badly as she (if what she'd said and how she'd behaved last night was true and he hoped it was) wanted him. However, that didn't mean he was going to let her off the hook. After all he couldn't be certain she wanted him right now after what had happened between them last night. And he couldn't help having the sneaking suspicion that after a couple of After Shocks what any man might have done for Elena.

After all Odin was up for it with Elena, and from what he'd seen, so was Elena with Odin.

So basically, what Marc needed to know this morning was where he stood with Elena.

Her eyes couldn't meet his, he noticed, with a mixture of annoyance and anxiety pooling low in his gut. She didn't ask him in, but opened the door wide and stepped back. So he supposed that meant enter.

His heavy hiking boots were thick with snow. He tugged the laces, toed them off, thumped them against the wall under her porch to remove hard packed snow from the soles and placed them on the mat to dry inside the door. Still not speaking, Elena closed the door and moved past him into the sitting room. He raised his brows, but said nothing as he stripped off his gloves and stuffed them in the pocket of his jacket, unwound his scarf, ski hat, hung them on a hook and moved to join her.

The sitting room looked different in daylight, bigger, but still warm and cozy.

There was a scent of cinnamon in the air, of Christmas and of yo-ho-ho.

Marc hadn't had a lot of yo-ho-ho in his life lately.

And he could only hope that Elena might provide some.

He was tired after a filthy sleepless night filled with a burning frustration that had eventually led him to down a couple of brandies.

They hadn't helped.

Nothing had helped.

His eyes scanned the room.

She'd tidied and dusted and the log burner was blazing away, throwing out welcome heat.

"Would you like a coffee, toast?" she asked in a soft voice that wobbled a little.

For some reason her demeanour, the heat flushing her cheeks, her neck, and way she was biting her bottom lip, made him feel a hell of a lot better.

She was a nervous wreck.

Well, that made two of them.

He couldn't remember feeling this nervous around a woman in his life.

When it came to seduction, normally he was the one in charge of the setting and of the end result.

But today Marc was on her turf, in her personal space.

Elena made the rules.

He took a steadying breath.

Okay, he could live with that.

And where was the confident, demanding girl from the night before?

The ache in his groin was still making its presence felt, but the tension in his belly, his shoulders, eased away.

He studied her as she reached up into the cupboard for an oversized mug with the little lilac flowers.

She was dressed from head to toe in black.

The colour of mourning.

God, she was beautiful.

Not all skin and bone like some women and a couple of the girls on reception or many who worked for the Ferranti Group.

Elena was tall, with a long line from head to toe, but under that huge sweatshirt she had breasts and hips and a stunning ass.

AN AFFAIR TO REMEMBER

Elena was a real woman. And in that dress she'd worn last night, she'd looked sensational.

But today it was as if there were two Elena's. The one who ran the busy reception of a first class hotel with humour and panache. The one last night who was mouthy with a hard-ass attitude. The one who knew what she wanted and how to get it. He liked that Elena. He liked her a lot.

And then there was this one, a little shy of herself and of him. A little unsure of herself and especially of him. He liked this Elena, too.

She turned to look at him, raised brows over wary eyes, and he realised he hadn't responded to her question if he wanted a drink.

"Yes, thanks. Black is fine. And I'll have toast if you're making it. Did you sleep well? No hangover?"

Her response to the little digs, (even though he'd asked nicely btw. After all, he was a *very nice* guy) was a tiny jerk of her chin that told him he'd scored a hit.

The mug was placed on the bump of a breakfast bar, which held two high stools. He slid onto one, settled himself, and picked up his coffee. He took a sip. Working for Nico Ferranti, Marc was used to nothing but the best. The coffee was very good. The girl had serious skills. A large bowl, same pattern as the mug, was filled with a selection of sliced fresh fruit and placed between them. Without a word, and without meeting his eye, she handed him a side plate, a knife and a large napkin of white cotton. No paper napkins for her. It seemed Elena had standards. Then she took a platter with a selection of cheeses from the fridge, placed it on the counter top between them, sat opposite him and dug in.

They ate in silence.

It wasn't a companionable silence, the air was too think with tension for that.

And all the while she focused on her food, her coffee.

And all the while Marc focused on her.

On how young she looked now she was outside her work environment. On the sprinkle of freckles on her nose. On how

51

astoundingly long her thick lashes were. How sweet her mouth looked. How gorgeous her clear skin was. How her ears hugged her skull. How her brows arched over wide eyes. On her pixie hair above a pixie face. He liked the whole package. He liked it a lot.

Now his gaze focused on the pulse beating like crazy wings beneath her ear.

And Marc decided to put her out of her misery.

"How are you feeling?"

Her insides churning, Elena placed her knife on top of her empty plate.

She needed to do something with her hands so she reached for her coffee, brought the mug to her mouth and watched him carefully over the rim.

Marc Atelier in his work uniform of Savile Row suit, crisp shirt of white cotton, fabulous silk tie and without a hair out of place, was something special. In a work environment, he had a reputation for fairness and straight talking. And for taking no prisoners.

Elena decided the Marc Atelier sitting opposite her was an unknown quantity.

With his dark brown hair all tousled after wearing his ski cap, he looked younger. The pale grey thermal sweater worn over a white T-shirt, sleeves shoved up to his elbows, brought out the blue of his eyes. She couldn't take her eyes off his spiky lashes as he studied her face the way she was studying his. He hadn't shaved and the dark shadow of his strong jaw only made him appear too handsome, if that was possible. On his wrist he wore a Breitling watch, black face, black leather strap. Unpretentious. Outrageously expensive. His blue jeans, ancient, comfortable, were slung low on his hips even as they hugged long and muscled thighs. She couldn't see the bulge between his legs since the breakfast bar blocked the view, but she knew it was there. Hard. Aroused. Ever ready.

It didn't matter what he wore, at the end of the day the man who sat opposite her was, to put it bluntly, a warrior. She came from a family of warriors herself, so Elena knew what she was talking about. He'd been in the military. She could see it in the steadiness of his eyes. In the strength of his wide jaw. In the way he sat, shoulders back and relaxed and comfortable in his own skin. He was a man at ease with himself and his surroundings. It pleased her that he could be at home in her home. And it felt right he was here, now, with her. Especially after the night before.

So, how *was* she feeling?

Good question.

It deserved an honest answer.

And something told her, his firm mouth perhaps, that Marc was not in the mood to be jerked around. The time had come for the truth, the whole truth, and nothing but the truth.

"I feel embarrassed and mortified that I might have put you in an uncomfortable situation last night. One not of your choosing. To be perfectly honest, I'm not used to hard liquor..."

His eyes stayed on her face as she took a break, took a tiny sip of coffee. She needed to take a breath or she'd be babbling like a fool. But she couldn't help the heat staining her cheeks.

"Perfectly understandable that you felt you needed a stiff drink. You'd had an upsetting evening. You had to deal with a very sick young man in front of everyone in a busy restaurant. Your boyfriend had been... unkind. Do you love him?"

Too right she'd had an upsetting evening.

Too right Tom had been unkind, he'd been horrible and he'd hurt her.

She'd no idea he'd had the power to hurt her.

The last question shocked her and she didn't know why.

It was a perfectly reasonable question.

So she gave it a perfectly reasonable answer.

"No. After last night I don't even like him. Usually, I stay friends with ex-boyfriends, but that's not going to happen with him."

"Good," Marc said. "But you must have seen something in him to go out with him in the first place."

Now Elena frowned into her coffee.

God, the man didn't know when to give up.

Oh well, she'd already made a complete ass of herself, what was one more humiliating moment?

"My brother set us up. He works with Tom. Thought we'd gel."

"Does your brother often organise your dates?"

Thinking of her big brothers, she had to smile.

And right there his blue eyes went dark as pitch, hungry.

The smile slid from her face as her mouth went too dry and her heart rate kicked.

"I have six brothers, all older than me. I'm the baby."

He blinked and the look in his eyes slid away as his brows rose into his hairline.

Elena had the distinct feeling she'd just dodged a speeding bullet.

"Six?"

"Yep."

He ran his tongue over the inside of his cheek.

A habit, she realised, something he did when he was trying hard not to smile.

"And what do your brothers do?"

She didn't miss the searching question in the question.

It was, should I be afraid?

Oh yeah, buddy.

Be very afraid.

It cost her, but she kept her face straight.

"Two policemen. An E.R. surgeon. Three in the military."

His face didn't exactly go pale, but she spotted the way he drew back, just a little.

"And every one very protective of their little sister."

It was a rhetorical question.

But she answered it anyway.

Elena leaned over the breakfast bar and all the while her eyes stayed on his.

"Better believe it, big boy."

The big boy tag had been a mistake, she knew it as soon as the words had left her stupid mouth. She knew it by the way he leaned back in the chair, by the way he folded strong arms, and by the way he spread his legs and especially by the way his eyes narrowed on hers.

AN AFFAIR TO REMEMBER

Shit.

"You said a lot of things to me last night, Elena. A lot of things." He paused. Oh God, she loved the way he called her Elena, all growly and deep. But what did that mean? That he was angry with her? While she was sitting here with her mind spinning out of control, he just sat there and studied the way her face went nuclear, the way her breath was panting too fast, and the way she was chewing her bottom lip.

Now he moved to lean his elbows on the counter top as his eyes pinned her to the spot.

"So what I want to know. No, strike that. What I *need* to know right now, is do you still feel the same way about me this morning?"

Chapter Nine

Hell, yeah!

Elena wanted to scream the words.

But a belated sense of self-preservation held her back.

What would happen if she said yes?

What if he walked away once she'd admitted her feelings?

But how likely was that, really?

Her whole body went on tingle alert, inside and out.

What was that old saying again? Nothing lost, nothing gained?

"Well," she said, and licked parched lips. Her eyes flew to his when he growled in his throat. And she took it as a clear warning to get on with it. "I did say that you make me tingle. And I can say, quite truthfully, that I'm tingling now."

The pupils in his eyes fully dilated, but his hard mouth went soft in a way that made her lick her lips again. His response was to stand and make his way around to her side. There was a hot rock lodged in her throat making it very hard for her to swallow. Very slowly, still sitting in her stool, she turned around to face him. His hands reached for her, cupped her face. And as soon as he touched her, her whole body went up in flames.

The outside world was eerily quiet as thick flakes of snow steadily drifted down from a heavy sky. All that could be heard was the crackle and hiss from the log burner and the frantic beat of her heart against her ribs.

Eventually Elena took a deep breath, she had to or she would have passed out.

He smelled amazing.

Shampoo, peppery cologne and aroused male.

Now his breath was on her mouth.

"Look at me."

Definitely a command.

She obeyed.

And her eyes rammed into his.

At that moment Elena felt as if she was falling into him, a sensation that was not only wonderful but terrifying, too. His eyes stayed on hers as he kissed her and she kissed him right back. His mouth was hard and soft and firm and smooth. When the tip of his tongue ran along her bottom lip and then her top lip, she opened her mouth and let him slide all the way inside. His tongue danced with hers, tempting, tasting, tantalising her senses. God, he was really, really good at this. And then his teeth tugged so, so gently on her bottom lip, pulling it before letting go. And then his tongue soothed the sting. She reciprocated the move, heard and felt his groan shudder through his big body. And now his hands pulled her close so that she was sitting right on the edge of the stool and set between his legs, his hard length pressing like steel into her belly. His head eased back, although his body stayed connected to hers. Now his hand slid up her shoulder, past her neck, to cup her face. His thumb rubbing her bottom lip as his eyes held hers in thrall.

"Touch me," he whispered. "Like you did last night."

Her breasts were heavy now, the nipples aching and throbbing with a need that matched the heavy liquid beat between her thighs. She knew she was slick and hot and swollen and scared stupid. And it would only get worse for her if she touched him. Nevertheless, her hand slid between them and she cupped him, pressed the flat of her hand against steel that her touch made grow. Now he was pulsing under her searching fingers. His cheeks were flushed, his eyes dark as his big body shuddered once, twice.

"Tell me," he whispered in a throat that was hoarse with need. "Do you still want me to do all those things to you?"

Elena hesitated to respond, and for a split second a flash of vulnerability entered those blue eyes. If she hadn't been staring right into them, she'd have missed it. As it was, it was gone so fast, she wondered if she'd imagined it. But that flash made her brave, made her take a risk, made her believe what she was doing was not wrong but so very right.

"I want you to do all those things, and more.... but..."

He kissed her hard, once.

And then he was staring into her eyes again.

"But, what, Sweetheart?"

Her eyes filled and she blinked frantically.

Now was so not the time to fall apart.

"I'm scared."

"That makes two of us," he admitted.

She read the sincerity in his denim blue eyes, in the husky tone of his voice.

"What's happening to us?"

His eyes searched hers as his thumb stroked her hot cheek.

"I think it's called a chemistry that's off the charts."

That made sense.

It was certainly something very special and very scary.

"Have you ever experienced anything like this before?"

She had to ask, if for no other reason than to try to understand.

He shook his head.

"Never. Will you trust me not to hurt you?"

Her lids fell, hiding her eyes.

"Last night," she said. "You must have been terribly frustrated, hurting. I'm so sorry, Marc."

"Look at me." Her lids rose and she saw a raw and ravaging need that almost took her breath. "I can't lie. I didn't sleep a wink last night. But you were under the influence of an alcohol you'd never had before. What sort of man would I be to take advantage of that?"

Now her hands rose to cup his face, to let her thumbs rub along the stubble of that strong jaw, that determined mouth.

"A good man." She kissed him on the mouth and then she pressed her body into his, relaxed, and surrendered to this good man.

Marc felt her yield to him.

Now her mouth was hungry on his as her desperate hands were tugging his thermal up. He dragged his mouth from hers to whip off his tops and then he moved to strip her. As her body was revealed, his breath caught in his throat. She wasn't wearing a bra.

His hands were shaking as he reached out to gently cup her swollen breasts. They were so firm, the skin so soft, like velvet wrapped in silk, as he tested their weight. Perfect. His thumbs stroked and flicked rosy nipples that beaded and pulsed. She threw her head back with a moan that vibrated through his body and arrowed right to his dick. The sting in his loins had him hiss out a breath. He'd never had a woman so responsive to his touch like this woman. Now her hands were at the buttons on his jeans, her eyes wide as she released him. He wasn't wearing underwear and was so fucking glad.

He helped her shove his pants past his knees and then he toed off his socks and tugged down her pants and panties as she kicked off her boots, her own socks.

And then they were standing in front of each other, their hands linked as they stared at each other, bare naked, for the very first time. She was beyond his wildest dreams. Her eyes were too wide, filled with a desire that made him want to weep with something like joy. Her mouth was trembling with each breath in and out. The hectic beat of her heart was fluttering in the pulse beneath her ear, against her ribs. He could see it and feel it as he held her hands tight. Her breasts were high, the tips reaching towards heaven. Her waist dipped and then flowed into lean hips, boyish. And then his gaze explored the swollen heat of her slick womanhood, tucked safely between the cut of her lean and long thighs right down past her calves to slim ankles and narrow feet. He knew she was doing the same thing to him. Checking him out. Her wide eyes spent a long, long time on his package. And his dick pulsed as it reached out searching relentlessly for its mate, her. His body seemed magnetised as it tilted towards hers.

He'd never felt anything like it.

At the edges of his mind, of his consciousness, he acknowledged the fluttering wings of fear. No fucking wonder. Because he knew instinctively that if he took her the way he wanted to, the way she wanted him to, both of them ran the risk of losing something that they might never get back.

The human heart was an organ that in some ways was stronger than titanium. But only if it gave love and received love

CC MACKENZIE

freely and unconditionally. And in other ways the human heart was as vulnerable as dragonfly wings. Hard words, feelings unspoken, or deception might shatter a heart into a thousand pieces and break a person apart emotionally and physically.

Marc knew this.

All the while his hands were learning, like Braille, every curve, every sensitive spot on that wondrous body that made her breath hitch, made her shudder, made her moan, his mind continued to debate, to give him a choice.

Give everything to this woman, without conditions.

Or take everything from her and give nothing back.

What was it to be?

Chapter Ten

Elena sensed the change in him.

He'd stopped stroking her when something like a sob had escaped from his throat.

She closed her eyes, pressed her forehead into his heaving chest, felt the heavy thud of his heart and just breathed through an arousal that was more pain than pleasure. His shaft was pressing, pressing into the soft flesh of her bare belly. God knew her body was ready, more than ready for him.

"What is it?" she whispered.

His hands stroked her back in a soothing rhythmic touch that did anything but soothe.

"I'm having a moment."

Now she rubbed her cheek against the light sprinkling of soft dark hair on the taut skin that covered his pectoral muscles. She smelled him, the scent of a clean aroused man. And Elena knew she'd recognise that scent anywhere, even if blindfold. Her hands continued to explore. Lord, he was built. She loved touching him, loved feeling the way his muscles tightened and then trembled under her searching fingers. She let her hands stroke up his strong back, over wide shoulders, before sliding down, down to massage his tight ass. His groan was neither pain nor pleasure. It was a bit of both.

Since they were taking a breather, Elena took the time to search her feelings and her heart to make sure both were good with what she wanted from him. The truth is always there if a person is open enough and honest enough to ask the right question of themselves at the right time. What did she want from him? And the answer was clear. She wanted it all, everything he could give. To be honest she'd known what she wanted as soon as she'd set eyes on him. As soon as he'd arrived at Ludlow Hall. He was a man who meant business. A genuine man. An honourable man. She wanted him in her life, for good. And if they were lucky, maybe even babies.

The enormity of where her heart was going hit Elena too hard.

Because she knew that in order to receive she needed to give, without strings, without a tie that bound him to her.

Now it was her turn to sob.

And Marc went utterly still under her hands.

"What is it?" he whispered.

Perhaps, Elena decided, they were both going a little bit crazy with the terribly potent sexual chemistry, all the pheromones, that were screwing around with their systems, their thought processes.

"I'm having a moment."

She had to laugh because lust had, in the space of a few minutes, turned into something else. Maybe it would have been better if he had taken her last night, when she was all relaxed and ready and wanting and willing.

Trust her to find a man with ethics and a strong moral compass.

Well, she'd opened up to him last night and he hadn't gone running for the hills.

Might as well tell him the rest of it.

"You're trembling," he said.

"I think we're stuck."

He eased back.

At least his upper body eased back, the rest of him was plastered against her.

His blue eyes were still dark as they studied her breast, as his knuckles stroked her swollen nipple. As if he couldn't help but touch her.

"Stuck?"

His mouth twitched as his tongue explored the inside of his cheek.

Her brows rose.

She was glad someone was finding it funny.

"I think maybe we want this too much. And it's a bit overwhelming."

He blinked.

"You're feeling overwhelmed?"

"Of course, aren't you?"

He dipped his head to rub his beard over her cheek.

"Baby," whispered in her ear, his voice harsh as he held her too tight. "I'm fucking terrified."

It wasn't so much the words, although they were definitely powerful. It was the tone. A tone filled with an agony that she could get behind since she felt it herself. And right there, Elena knew that someone needed to take the lead, so it might as well be her.

After all, what did she have to lose?

Plenty.

"You're trembling again," he muttered in her ear as he just stood there and hung onto her.

Now she was the one to ease back, to hold his face between her hands, to look deep into those blue eyes.

"I think I've fallen madly in love with you. I've never said those words to a man before. Except to my dad and my brothers. But they don't count at the moment. I love you and I'm really scared. Because if this goes to hell, then I don't know if I'll ever recover."

She wanted to ask him if there was a chance he might love her, too.

But that wasn't what love was all about.

It wasn't about I love you so you'd better love me back.

He shook his head.

And just like that her heart dropped to land with a sickening thud at her feet.

And she shut her eyes tight because she didn't want to hear it.

Then his mouth was on hers, coaxing her to open. With a sob in her throat and a heart that felt like it was shattering into a thousand pieces, she gave him everything.

He was breathing heavily by the time he lifted his head to stare into her swimming eyes.

"You humble me. I've seen bravery in Iraq, in Afghanistan. I've seen men and women risk their own life for others. But you, you are the bravest person I know. And I'm falling madly in love with you, too. I feel like I'm about to jump out of my skin, but I love you so much it hurts. It hurts me, Elena."

And then she was scooped up in his arms, as if her weight didn't matter. Which was nothing more than an illusion because Elena knew she wasn't a light weight. She threw her arms around his neck as he stumbled up the narrow stairs.

"Jeez, these stairs are going to kill me," he muttered against her hungry mouth.

By the time he staggered into her bedroom and dumped her on her bed, she was laughing her head off. She leaned on her elbows and raised her brows as she watched him fist himself and stroke his length.

"What happened to being bent over the arm of the sofa and being taken hard and fast?"

His smile split his face in a way that she'd never seen before.

He was happy.

And her heart soared.

"I thought we might start with the basics first. I want to see your eyes when I make you mine, when you come."

In spite of having central heating, the room had a chill to it, plus they were naked. Now Elena pulled back the comforter and welcomed him in.

They lay on their sides under the comforter, all warm and snug and facing each other, not speaking, just staring into each other's eyes.

"Why do you keep stroking yourself? Shouldn't that be my job?" she said.

His smile made her tummy flip.

"I'm trying to calm the beast. It's been a while for me."

"Don't you want to take the edge off?"

"I'm a gentleman. The lady should come first."

She grinned and moved in closer, her mouth within kissing distance of his.

AN AFFAIR TO REMEMBER

Placing little nips of her teeth and little licks of her tongue on his mouth, her hand slid down to cover his and then lower to cradle his balls. The groan that escaped from his throat coincided with his full body shudder.

In a flash she was under him, long legs wrapped around his hips, her arms holding him close. Her hand thrust through his hair, her nails scratching his scalp as the steel of his shaft slid up and down her wet, slick heat, teasing her until she sighed.

"I want to taste you." Was all the warning she received as he took a long, lingering journey down her torso, taking his own sweet time to torment and torture her nipples. Then he loitered at her belly button, using his tongue to taste and tease. His nose nuzzled the tender skin between hip and thigh as strong hands slid under her bottom, lifted her core to his mouth.

She waited and waited for him to touch her... there.

By the time he'd kissed and licked and tasted everywhere but... there, she was crying his name. Then the lips of her sex were spread and he used the flat of his tongue to lick again and again. He used his tongue as a weapon of pleasure, spearing it inside her. But when he sucked the swollen bead of her clitoris, gently used his teeth, she flew apart.

And it wasn't the end because now two fingers entered her, stretching her wide as he searched to find the spot he was looking for and used those fingers ruthlessly to bring her screaming to peak yet again. Then she was hauled to the edge of the bed, her legs over his shoulders as he grabbed her hips and took her, made her his, with one hard thrust. Her shocked inhale didn't stop him as his hips pistoned hard and fast, as her breasts bounced with each impalement. She was on her back with nothing to hold onto. So she held on tight to the sheets, fisting her hands as he went faster and faster. The friction was something she'd never experienced before as her body climbed higher and higher. But it was the expression on his face that held her captive, she couldn't look away. His eyes were dark and burned into hers as his brow creased as his white teeth were bared with something that looked more like pain than pleasure. And she knew he was battling to hold on until she flew, but she couldn't quite get there. One hand released her to slide between her legs as his thumb moved to the spot where his body joined hers and he found that swollen button and worked it as hard as he was working her. When her back and her neck arched that was when he let go. He fell upon her, held her close and cried her name as his seed shot into her again and again.

Marc just had to close his eyes and try to breathe through what her body was doing to his. Still her core gripped his dick, squeezing and milking him dry. His lungs were heaving as he made a pitiful attempt to suck air. Their hearts were racing and they were covered in healthy sweat and still her body refused to release him.

"Don't move," he begged.

Her soft laugh actually vibrated right through his dick, he'd never felt anything like it in his life.

"Don't laugh either or you'll kill me."

Her response was a slow slide of her hand from his shoulder to his ass and back again. He reckoned it was supposed to be a soothing motion. To his dick it was anything but and when her hand lingered on his ass and squeezed and then ran her nails over it, his body twitched in appreciation. Like a contented kitten, she purred deep in her throat and he had to clench his teeth.

"If you say one word," he warned.

"I'm not the one doing all the talking," she whispered.

"I think you've broken the beast."

Now she did laugh and laughed harder when he swore and slid out of her.

Chapter Eleven

The following Monday afternoon Marc sat in a plush leather chair opposite Nico Ferranti in Nico's office at his home, The Dower House, rather than Nico's office in Ludlow Hall.

"I am thinking we should remove the bugs. It is impossible to get any work done," Nico said.

Nico was an impressive looking man, tall, lean and dark as befitted his Italian heritage. Marc was used to seeing Nico looking immaculate in hand-crafted suits from Savile Row. He rarely saw him dressed as he was today, in jeans tucked into boots and a cashmere sweater.

"We still don't know who the mole is," Marc reminded him.

"*Si*, I know this, but I try to keep my home and professional life separate."

Family time was important to Nico, Marc understood that, admired it even.

"We've managed to narrow down the list of suspects to two. One from the reception staff and one from housekeeping."

Now Nico leaned across the desk, his grey eyes sharp.

"Who?"

Marc had been expecting this reaction.

"I don't want to say until we have facts and proof. It's crucial that there is no change in your habits or demeanour towards the staff when you're working. The last thing we want to do is to scare him or her off. Just give us another few days. We've placed hidden cameras in your office, in reception's back office and in housekeeping."

Nico scratched his chin and didn't look happy.

"It is a great pity we cannot think of a way to flush them out."

Marc ran his tongue inside his cheek and Nico spotted the tic.

"Have you thought of something?"

Actually, he had.

But it was very risky and might cause more trouble than it was worth.

He also needed to come clean about a personal matter.

"I'm seeing Elena Kennedy, in a personal capacity."

Nico blinked.

"She is a lovely girl. Is it serious?"

"Yep."

Now Nico grinned, wiggled his dark brows.

"How serious?"

Marc didn't flinch from telling him the truth.

Nico Ferranti was not only his employer, he was also his very good friend.

"Marriage, babies, the whole happy ever after."

Marc rose as Nico got to his feet, strolled around the desk to envelope him in a Nico Ferranti speciality, the man hug. He was kissed once on each cheek, hugged tight and given a back slap that would fell a bull elephant.

"*Congratulazioni*! I am happy, happy, for you and Elena. She comes from a large *famiglia* of good men. *Un momento*!" Nico strode to the door, opened it and yelled, "Bronte, *bella*!"

"What's up, babe?" came the response from the vast family kitchen, living room

"Bring champagne and three glasses. We have a *celebrazioni*!"

"Oooooooh! Coming right up."

Nico rubbed his hands as he strolled back to sit behind his desk, his handsome face split with a wide grin, his grey eyes dancing with delight. His friend's sincere pleasure in Marc's personal happiness was a gift that he never took for granted.

Bronte Ferranti entered carrying a bottle of the very best champagne wrapped in a folded white napkin and three champagne glasses. She kissed her husband on the mouth, handed him the champagne, placed the glasses on the desk and turned to Marc.

"Hey, Marc."

She held out her arms and Marc was only too delighted to give her a hug.

AN AFFAIR TO REMEMBER

Bronte was willow slim and as tall as Elena.

But where Elena was dark, Bronte was light.

She was a natural ash blonde with wide emerald eyes, creamy skin, high cheekbones and a full mouth. The only jewellery she wore was a slim wedding band of white gold set with tiny diamonds. The Ferranti's did not flash the cash. Today she wore black skinny jeans, a pale grey polo neck sweater of fine cashmere and her shining head of hair was tied back in a complicated plait. Bronte Ferranti was drop dead gorgeous. And she had a heart of solid gold, something else she shared with Elena.

Nico popped the cork.

"Hey, yourself," Marc said. "I hope we haven't put you out. Where are the kids?"

Bronte shook her head, patted his cheek and accepted a glass from her husband before settling herself into the chair next to Marc and crossed endless legs.

"The twins are attending a birthday party and nanny's bathing Eve. Anyway, you could never put me out." Bronte grinned at the two men. "Okay, don't keep me in suspense, guys. What are we celebrating?"

"Marc is in love."

Bronte's eyes grew as wide as her smile as she turned to Marc.

"Really?" she asked, rolling the 'r' in a way that made him look to heaven. "Who is she? Anyone we know?"

"Elena Kennedy," Marc said before Nico could beat him to it.

If anything Bronte's smile went even wider.

"I adore Elena. She's full of fun. I'm so pleased for both of you. When did this happen?"

"Friday night. Although I've had my eye on her for a while."

"You must bring her to dinner," Nico said. "We will make a plan."

"How are you settling in?" Bronte wanted to know, referring to the A frame cottage he'd been given. The place was stunning. And with five bedrooms was probably too big for one man. But that was Nico Ferranti for you, generous to a fault.

"Love it," he said, sincerely.

"I've been thinking," Bronte said. "Why don't you bring your mother and Nina up to stay with you over the holiday season? And beyond if you want to. I know that the first Christmas after I lost my parents was incredibly hard. Maybe the change of scene is just what your mother needs."

Actually Marc had been thinking of doing just that. His adopted parents had been married for over forty years. It was only natural that Mary Jones was struggling to come to terms with her loss. However, Nina was worried that her mother was sinking into depression. Losing a loved one was a time when family pulled together. Closing the large house in Devon wouldn't be a problem either.

"Do you need a bigger cottage?" Nico wanted to know.

Marc didn't think so, but Bronte jumped in.

"What about Heron's Rest? It's fully completed and tested and looking amazing." She turned to Marc. "It would be perfect because it's a double A frame with a single story kitchen living space with covered deck linking the two frames. It would mean Nina and Mary would have their own private living space and you would have yours."

Marc shook his head.

"It has eight bedrooms."

But Bronte was not to be deterred.

"Yes, but you'll need office space to do your spook stuff. Nina needs a place to study, too. And it's the perfect place for a Christmas party. Don't forget Elena has a large family. It's perfect!"

Marc felt as if he was being run over by a gentle steamroller. He looked helplessly at Nico for assistance, but his friend was grinning from ear to ear.

"*Si*, it is sorted."

The sound of a child's wail from upstairs had Bronte springing to her feet.

"Time for a feed before bed. No, please don't get up," she said, when Marc went to rise. "Tell Elena I'll be in touch. See you later." And she was gone.

Nico couldn't stop grinning at Marc's shell-shocked face.

"She is weaning Eve, the *bambino* still needs to be close to her *mama*."

"You have a beautiful family, Nico."

Now the big Italian's grey eyes went soft.

"*Si*, we are lucky men. People like us, people who have known hunger, pain. It is not often we are given a chance to have a life like this. *Evviva*, Marc. You have done well with your life, for your sister and now for your *mama*. I am proud to be your friend."

And that was Nico Ferranti all over.

The Italian wore his heart on his sleeve and could make a grown man weep.

As Nico topped up their glasses, Marc sat forward, prepared to lay out his idea to catch a betrayer in the act.

"So, about the mole," he said, and sat back to enjoy his wine. "I have a plan."

Chapter Twelve

It was one week until Christmas and Elena was supervising the large reception area at Ludlow Hall. And she'd never been happier.

Was it possible that being madly in love with the man of her dreams made a woman skinny? More than one person had mentioned that she looked different and that she looked as if she'd lost weight. She grinned, probably all the multiple orgasms she was having. A wall in her office had one way glass so that she could keep an eye on the comings and goings. Now she moved to a long wall mirror and made sure her two piece suit, made of the finest Italian wool the colour of a cappuccino, was still sharp. Nico Ferranti had brought in a design team to tailor the uniforms for all Ferranti front line staff. And Elena loved the way the cut flattered everyone. Each staff member had eight pieces to choose from; skirts, pants, three jacket styles and dresses. There were uniforms for summer and winter, too. But it was the shoes that Elena absolutely adored. Smart pumps of chocolate brown leather handmade in Italy that matched an optional slim shoulder bag. Today Elena's jacket had a Mandarin collar, the jacket tailored to nip in at the waist and to skim just below her bottom, and the skirt was slim with a kick pleat at the back. She wore a chocolate brown scarf of the finest silk at her neck with gold F's embossed for Ferranti.

She took a breath and strolled out of her office to take over desk duty for thirty minutes.

"Time to take a break, Jenny. You've done very well today. Are you enjoying yourself?"

Jenny was nineteen, fresh from the local college and an enthusiastic addition to the team.

She turned to Elena and grinned, her eyes thrilled with the pat on the back.

"I love working here, Elena."

"Good to hear."

"Evening, ladies."

The deep voice had Elena's cheeks burn, but she kept calm and turned to give Marc a strictly professional smile. Shame she could do nothing about the happiness glittering in her hazel eyes or the tingles that raced through her system giving her gooseflesh.

Even little Jenny wasn't immune to the Marc Atelier affect.

"Good evening, Mr. Atelier," she breathed.

The girl's eyes were huge as she looked her fill over a wonderful example of prime male real estate.

"Thirty minutes, Jenny," Elena reminded her, shaking her head as the girl headed for the break-out area.

"What time do you finish?"

Elena turned to eye a Marc who was looking immaculate in his dark suit, crisp white shirt and dark tie. He had a tiny earpiece in his left ear and a slim walkie talkie slipped into the top pocket of his jacket.

"One hour. The evening shift are due in thirty minutes." She turned to squint out the windows to see fat snowflakes falling, and added, "Weather permitting."

"The roads have been ploughed and we have our own team keeping the entrance, the drive and the paths clear," he paused to stare at her mouth in a way that made her pulse kick. He'd been giving her that look all day. Now his eyes met hers and what she saw there made her mouth dry.

"Why don't I take your key and prepare for... dinner?"

His voice was low and the tone promised a lot more than... dinner.

The tingles were now a steady buzz through her system.

Her, "Okay," was a breathy whisper. Under the circumstances, that was the best she could manage.

One of the simple pleasures that they'd discovered together was the preparation of food.

Marc had been taught to cook by the wonderful Mary Jones, a woman Elena had talked to at length on the phone, but hadn't met. And Elena was no slouch in the kitchen herself.

She popped into her office to grab her keys and turned to find him right behind her.

"You're very sneaky." The glint in his eye made her slap her hand to his wide chest. "No kissing in the office."

Too late.

He landed a hard kiss on her stunned mouth as he whipped her keys from her hand.

"Text me if you're delayed," he said and sauntered out.

Elena tried, really tried, to be annoyed with him, but it didn't work.

A curl of excitement uncoiled deep in her belly, along with a sense of anticipation.

She couldn't wait.

Marc let himself into the coach house, turned off the alarm.

After a verbal tussle that had ended with sex on the floor, he'd managed to get his way about Elena arming the security system and educating her about the importance of an entry and exit routine to help keep her safe.

The house smelled of Elena he thought as he hung his coat on the hook.

He stripped off his jacket, tie and unbuttoned his shirt, as he made his way upstairs to the space he already thought of as 'their' bedroom. Stepping out of his shoes, he made short work of his pants and folded them over the back of a chair, hung up his jacket like a good boy. Elena liked order in her life, so he picked up his Calvin's, socks, and tossed them in the laundry. Padding over the floor, he turned on a bedside light and closed the curtains. And headed for the shower.

The architect who'd overseen the conversion of the coach house had sacrificed a third second floor bedroom to construct an awesome walk-in shower and bath arrangement. Marc and his woman had enjoyed shower sex this morning and he couldn't wait to do it again... along with other... things.

Every time he thought of Elena Kennedy he went rock hard, just like that. He'd never felt like this about a woman before, love, affection and wicked lust all rolled into one. He'd been a horny bastard all day. Now he lifted his head to the power of water steaming from a shower head the size of a dinner plate and just let it rinse away, not only soap and shampoo, but the cares and stresses of the day.

He grabbed a towel from the heated rail, wound it around his waist and ignored the way his dick made it tent at the front, the penalty for thinking about shower sex and Elena. Using another towel to dry his hair, he turned and saw the woman herself leaning against the bathroom door frame and enjoying the view.

He grinned.

"Hey, baby. You're early."

In the light, her hazel eyes were a glowing gold as they took a long look at his pecs, his belly and then lingered on a part of him that seemed to have a mind of its own around her these days.

"The evening crew arrived early so I took advantage and left early." She licked her lips and the tent pole grew. Now her eyes flicked to his and he read more than desire in those golden eyes, he read hunger, he read need. "And I can see you're very happy to see me," she said in a hoarse whisper.

There were times when Marc liked his sex a little bit rough and a little bit hard. So far, he hadn't introduced Elena to his likes and dislikes. At all times his first priority was seeing to her needs, her happiness. Plus, he'd been having too much fun learning the secrets of her body, inside and out. But then he remembered the things she'd told him under the influence of After Shock. Things like having her panties at her ankles, things like having him bend her over the arm of the sofa, things like taking her from behind fast and hard.

He could do all that and more.

No problemo.

"Why don't you get out of that uniform," he suggested, in a low voice that was more of a purr than a growl. Those golden eyes went wide as she received the message. Had it only been a week since he'd first made love with her? Now all it took was a single look that scorched his soul, or a single lick of the lips that made his heart beat too fast. It was amazing how in tune they were with each other's needs, each other's desires.

She stripped off her nifty silk scarf, and Marc wondered if she was like most other women and owned a vast supply of scarves because he could put a number of them to good use. The jacket came next, showcasing a boned bra that was nothing more than a scrap of lace and silk and then she unzipped her skirt and his mouth went dry. The matching string panties hardly covered her smooth mound. When she turned her back to bend over to pick up her skirt he nearly embarrassed himself. Little tease. Now, she carefully hung up her suit in the closet. Instead of shoes she was wearing snow boots, so she sat on the edge of the bed and bent down to unzip her boots, giving him a fabulous view of smooth breasts. Tossing the boots aside, she stood before him in bra and panties, in all her glory, her eyes on his mouth as she lifted her chin.

A challenge.

He just loved a challenge.

By this time he'd dumped the towels.

Now he raised his hands to grip the top of the bathroom door frame and let her have a nice long and lingering look at a throbbing dick that was about to go nuclear.

"Like what you see, baby?" he purred.

Those golden eyes flicked to his and he saw them change colour to dark hazel as she licked her lips. Oh yeah, his baby more than liked it.

"If I promise to keep my hands where they are, would you like a taste?"

They'd indulged in plenty of oral play and he'd learned that Elena didn't like his hands on her head controlling the speed or the depth. And he respected her limits. Now he was placing himself in her hands, so to speak, and he hoped he could take their play to a whole new level.

Her hands went to the bra clasp behind her back.

"Leave it."

A dark brow rose at the command in his voice, but she did as he asked and didn't touch her panties either. She was a fast learner.

But she did grab a pillow from the bed and tossed it at his feet before she dropped to her knees. To steady herself, she grabbed his thighs and pressed her fingertips into his flesh.

Now Marc looked down into her face.

Her eyes were glued to his as her tongue flicked once, twice, over the too-sensitive head of his penis.

"Spread your legs... that's it... wider."

God, her thighs were lean and long and he could see the crotch of her ivory silk panties grow wet.

"Cup me, baby."

She did as he asked, weighing his heavy and swollen testicles and gave a deliciously careful squeeze of his balls. He hissed out a hot breath and all the time her eyes were on his.

"Suck me."

Her lids dropped a little as she nuzzled his length with her nose and inhaled. Her tongue licked one side of his length from bottom to the top as if he was her favourite popsicle, and then she did the same to the other side. Her other hand slid up the back of the tense muscle of his thigh to grip his ass hard. Only then did she take him in her mouth, only then did the tip of her tongue explore the sensitive spot just under the head of his penis and flick, flick, flick, until his whole body was shuddering. The hand cupping his balls now gripped the root of him and pumped. He was a big man, no way could she swallow him. But unexpectedly she took the tip of him to the back of her throat and swallowed.

He jerked as if electrified, his legs trembling.

Christ, what had he been thinking?

If he gripped the doorframe any harder he was going to break it.

And all the while her eyes stayed fixed on his face, watching his response to every single move of her wicked mouth and a tongue that was death by teasing. When he grew bigger, when his balls went hard, she released him and sat back on her heels, her beautiful face flushed, her lips swollen and those golden eyes glowing with satisfaction.

His dick was leaking and throbbing now.

Her hand reached out, she swiped a finger over the clear fluid, placed her finger in her mouth and sucked.

"Hmm, salty, nice."

His heart was threatening to escape from the cage of his ribs.

Okay, she liked how he tasted, that was good, that was cool.

He released his death grip on the door frame and hauled her to her feet and kissed her breathless. The kiss was hard, all tongue and teeth. By the time he released her, her eyes were huge and her breath was coming fast.

"Strip."

No hesitation, not even a second, and she was naked in front of him.

"Downstairs." When she blinked, he raised his brows and growled, "Now!"

Chapter Thirteen

Elena hadn't been expecting to find a cave-man in her house, in her bedroom tonight. A cave-man who was right on her heels as she slowly stepped down stairs. Her cheeks were burning with something more than embarrassment, more like a cocktail of self-consciousness and shyness. This was the first time she'd ever walked around naked in her own home. It took a bit of getting used to. And she was desperately trying to remember if she'd closed the sitting room curtains when she'd arrived. When they walked into the room she released a very big sigh of relief. The only light in the room came from the log burner and now her cave-man strolled over to light a couple of fat candles that smelled of cinnamon and apple, smelled of Christmas. Excitement and anticipation licked through her system, something told her that she was about to receive a present she'd never forget.

All thoughts, all worries fled from her mind because the cave-man grabbed her, his hand gripping her neck as he brought his hungry mouth down on hers and fed as if he hadn't been kissed for months. Actually this wasn't a kiss, it was more than that, much more. His hands used her ruthlessly, on her breast his fingers pinched her nipple, winding her body too high, too fast. His hand was between her legs now, forcing them apart, his fingers searching, seeking and spreading her slick heat over a swollen clitoris. He was taking possession of her as if he had every right to kiss her like this, to touch her like this.

And Elena loved it.

Then she couldn't think at all as every nerve end went tight, as she arched her back, as she dragged her mouth from his to scream his name as his fingers pumped into her tossing her over a cataclysmic orgasm that liquefied her very bones.

She was lifted from her feet and for a moment her hot face was buried in the slick heat of his neck where his carotid artery was pumping blood too fast.

Oh God, he was just as affected by all this as she was.

Now she was on her feet and he held her tight, his shaft like steel wrapped in velvet, pressing against her belly. His mouth took hers once more in a kiss that branded her as his.

He turned her around to stand near the wide arm of the sofa.

Omigod he was going to make a hot dream come true.

He bent her torso over the arm, a move that brought her bare bottom high in the air. With strong hands on her hips, he positioned her just right, until she was on her tip toes. Now those hands held her in a firm grip to keep her still as his thigh moved her legs apart, wider and wider again.

She tried to look over her shoulder, to see his face, anything, to give her a point of reference, but the room was too dark. Her hands gripped the sides of the seat cushion and held on tight. Everything that had happened to her, was happening to her, took on an almost dreamlike quality.

"Safe word," he snapped.

Safe word?

Why on earth would she need a safe word?

The palm of his hand connected hot and hard on her bare bottom.

The yelp was a combination of shock and alarm.

"Aftershock!" she cried.

His hand was rubbing the burning heat on her bottom in a way that made her whimper into the cushion.

"If I hurt you or you want me to stop you use the word. Say yes."

"Yes."

His exhale was unsteady and it told Elena he was just as turned on by all this as she was.

"Okay, baby. Brace yourself."

She did.

The expected thrust of entry didn't happen.

AN AFFAIR TO REMEMBER

Instead the throbbing head of his penis stilled over her pulsing clitoris and simply held.

She blinked.

It was the most amazing sensation. Her body was expecting hard and fast and received slow and slick. Her tingles went into tingling overdrive. Every nerve end from her scalp to her toes simply pulsed in time with the pressure his penis applied to *the spot*. Slowly and ever so gently his hands spread her buttocks apart as his thumbs slicked lower to spread the lips of sex wide and now he pressed himself into every part of her and all the while the slit of his penis opened to kiss her clit. The feeling that grew and grew and grew was warm and wet as the ache melted into a pleasure so deep it made her weep, but she couldn't come. Completion remained tantalisingly out of reach.

Now his big body was trembling right along with hers.

"Breathe through it, sweetheart. That's it... breathe, baby... breathe."

She breathed.

With every breath she took her womb went tighter and tighter, until a warm honey bathed their conjoined flesh. Her clitoris grew longer and swollen as an orgasm the likes of which she'd never dreamed of grew from her centre and soared her up, up, up and away.

Elena's eyes were closed.

She was naked, on her back on the sofa, warm and safe in her lover's strong arms.

He'd covered them in a throw.

Her legs were tangled in his.

His cheek was resting on top of her head.

She smelled soap, man and a combination of her sex and his.

It was a heady combination.

Elena lifted her head to gaze up into a face she'd never get tired of looking at.

Candle light flickered over that face, giving a dark and broody look as he stared into flames licking wood in the burner.

"You didn't come."

"Tonight isn't about me. Did you like it?"

Her response was to lick his neck.

Salty.

"I'll take that as a yes."

"You, Mr. Atelier, have serious skills."

"I've never done that with anyone else," he said.

She believed him.

It wasn't the words, it was the tone and it was the way he held her so close.

As if, to him, she was the most precious thing in the world to him.

Elena was slowly beginning to realise that being the recipient, lucky her, of this man's love was a wondrous thing.

"Believe me when I tell you that I'm feeling all warm and glowy. But is it fair for you to hold me like this when you must be hurting? There's something long and hard, very hard, laying against my hip."

Now he shifted to look down at her.

A smile teased his mouth, danced in his eyes.

"Will we be keeping count, then, sweetheart? I give you two orgasms, you give me two back. Is that how it's going to be?"

She blinked and then her eyes searched his face for... something.

He didn't look annoyed with her.

He didn't sound annoyed with her.

But she was quite certain he *was* annoyed with her, maybe a little.

When he put it like that, she was annoyed at herself.

Her brow creased and he placed his lips on the spot, left a kiss.

"No. I hear what you're saying. And you're right." Now her eyes flew to his, held. "But I don't want to be selfish either. Know what I mean?"

His smile showcased white teeth, crinkled the skin around his dark blue eyes.

"Don't worry about it. You're the least selfish person I know."

AN AFFAIR TO REMEMBER

Her mouth went on a slow journey of exploration over his strong jaw. When she set her teeth there, she found herself flat on her back and looking up into a face she was coming to know as well as her own.

"I love your mouth," she said, studying its beauty as her thumb rubbed his bottom lip.

"I love yours, but it's your eyes that get me every single time."

She fluttered her eyelashes, making him smile.

"My eyes?"

"They're the window to the soul. And you," he kissed her once before easing back, "have a beautiful soul."

She wiggled her hips to get the position just right, then her legs were around his backside, her heels kicked and he slid right in where he belonged.

"Oooooooh." Her back arched as he filled her, stretched her. "That feels soooooo good."

Now he grabbed her leg behind the knee and pushed it up and to the side, exposing the part where they were joined. His gaze slid down her body, he bit his bottom lip.

"You," he said between his teeth as he thrust hard once, twice. "Are one demanding woman."

Her glittering eyes shone bright with her love for him.

"Harder. Faster."

His breath hissed out as he did as she asked, his hips pumping as he pushed her knee higher.

Elena lifted her arms until her hands could grip the arm of the sofa and hold on tight. The purchase meant she could pump her hips in time with his. The friction became hot, became hard as each battled for domination. She'd asked for hard and fast, and by god he was giving it to her. Now his face tightened, his head was thrown back, the corded muscles in his strong neck went tight as he swore, then grunted her name again and again. Her core claimed him in an iron fist that clenched and at the same time perspiration beaded on his forehead, on his top lip. Her core clenched and released again and again and that's when she saw him bare his teeth before he pistoned into her, utterly out of control. His arms were trembling now and her knee was almost at her chin.

83

The thought entered her head that it was a good job she did yoga twice a week.

Then his eyes went too wide as his mouth made the O shape and his whole body went rigid. His seed shot inside her, bathing her womb, again and again. And a secret part of her wished that they'd made a baby this night. Because the child would most certainly be someone very special. A child made in unconditional love. The thought made his face swim as she watched his big body shudder again and again. And still her body refused to release him. Now his eyes caught hers and held. She saw the moment he registered her tears. Saw the love. And saw the anxiety, the worry, for her.

Never in her whole life had she had someone care for her so completely.

And now the tears fell faster.

His hand was shaking as he tried to wipe her cheeks.

"Baby, sweetheart, did I hurt you?"

She shook her head, grabbed his face between her hands and brought his head down for a kiss.

"No. I was just having a moment."

Apparently the kiss didn't convince him he'd done nothing wrong, his dark eyes searched hers.

"Are those good tears or bad tears?"

She sniffed, blinked frantically.

"Happy, happy tears."

Now his cheek was rubbing against hers and she knew she'd have a bad case of razor burn if he kept it up.

"I can't bear it when you cry. Please don't cry."

"I'll be crying for real if you keep rubbing your cheek on my face. It's like sandpaper."

He shifted his weight to the side, to stare down into her face.

"You hungry?"

"Starving."

He rose and lifted her in his arms.

As he moved towards the stairs, she bit her lip as he dinged his elbow against the wall, the curse made her bite her lip harder. He didn't put her down until they were in the shower.

AN AFFAIR TO REMEMBER

She braced herself for the sting of icy water before it warmed. They didn't speak until they were squeaky clean.

"I didn't realise you had a cave-man hiding inside."

He was smiling as he towel dried her hair.

"You liked it?"

"Is the Queen a girl?"

He was still laughing when they shared a bottle of wine with bowls of steaming pasta.

As she sat in her kitchen watching the expressions cross his face as he told her about his day and she told him about hers, learning more about how they ticked, a part of her stood outside the scene, looking in and simply watched them.

A part of her that prayed what they'd found together could last.

A part of her that prayed the real world with all its challenges might leave them alone, for a little while, to just enjoy the magic of two people who'd found each other and had fallen in love.

In the days and hours that followed, Elena would come to wish with all her heart they never left that little cottage in the snow.

Chapter Fourteen

The day from hell started like any other.

Elena skipped into her office, on top of the world.

Her heart was singing and her system was buzzing on a cocktail of love and hot sex.

Who needed food?

Christmas cheer was everywhere a person looked.

The weather, for once, was being kind with a light frost and no new falls of snow forecast for four days, which meant the roads were clear. The snow gritters had spread sand and salt on the car parks and the paths.

The reception staff were on top of their game.

Elena beamed benevolently on them and they, especially little Jenny, beamed right back at her.

The four year old Ferranti twins, Luca and Sophia stood holding Nico's hands as they stared with eyes like saucers at the tree.

The twenty foot Christmas tree in the grand foyer of the entrance to Ludlow Hall was decorated in creams and gold twinkling in thousands of ivory lights. The whole place smelled of Christmas with vast clear vases crammed with fresh oranges with cloves pressed into the peel. Christmas music warbled through the sound system, background noise to the ring of phones, the chatter of people, couples, families, all coming together to celebrate the holiday in style. The guests munched on hot mince pies, brandy and coffee.

The first inkling that Elena received that all was not well, was when two uniformed police officers were escorted by Marc Atelier and his team into Nico's office. The bellboys, the reception staff all looked at each other and shrugged. Maybe someone had been caught stealing from a car or even the rooms. It was very rare that a thief would take the chance to venture into Ludlow Hall because the word had gone out that Nico Ferranti took no prisoners. But it was Christmas time with rich pickings, so maybe the temptation had been too much and someone had decided to chance their arm.

Elena didn't think any more of it and instructed her team to, "Look sharp."

Fifteen minutes later she took a call from Alexander Ludlow telling her her presence was required in Nico's office. The summons was unexpected because reception was incredibly busy with new arrivals. Elena passed the baton to her number two. Everyone knew the police were still in Nico's office, so the speculative looks she received were unwelcome. Even little Jenny looked pale when Elena moved past her to enter the suite of rooms that protected the inner sanctum of Nico Ferranti's office.

Elena's heart beat a little faster as she knocked the door, heard the clipped, "Enter."

She opened the door.

Nico sat behind his desk, his face like a thundercloud preparing to drop hail on a lovely day. Alexander Ludlow was sitting on a long sofa next to Nico's PA, Julie, who had a pad and a pen in her hand.

The two policemen, she recognised Chief Inspector Andy Bradshaw, were standing next to two members of the security team and Marc. A Marc who didn't meet her eye. And for the first time alarm bells rang loud and clear in Elena's brain.

"Sit," Nico said, indicating a slim chair with no arms in front of his desk.

Elena's hands were suddenly clammy and a trickle of cold sweat slid relentlessly down her spine. Mind racing, wondering what the hell was the matter, and what it had to do with her, Elena blinked into Nico's face.

"Perhaps you would care to explain this?"

Nico pushed a file towards her.

Elena's brow creased as she picked up the file with hands that weren't quite steady.

Over the next ten minutes, ice pooled in her gut as she read message after message sent to someone called Tabitha Crew

(Elena had never heard of the woman) with varying degrees of personal information on the Ferranti's. Everything from what sort of treatments Bronte and her friends had at the spa, to who the couple met for dinner, with whom they had coffee, who they were close to, plus other little drips of information on Alexander and Rosie Ludlow, too.

A trembling hand brushed hair back from her face. Elena couldn't believe what she was reading. But the worst thing about it all was that every single message had been sent from *her* office computer on dates and times when *she* had been on duty.

The room spun as something like panic rose into her throat, buzzed in her ears.

No one spoke.

And the silence was deafening.

The silence was terrifying.

Elena shook her head.

She lifted her face to look Nico right in the eye.

"I would never, ever, do such a thing. Ever. I've never seen theses before. They're disgusting."

Nico didn't flinch, didn't blink.

"Very well. Perhaps you will be happy to help the police with their enquiries, be prepared to answer a few questions?"

Marc didn't say a single word.

She couldn't look at him.

"I am happy to help the police and you, Nico, in any way I can."

Police Inspector Andy Kershaw moved into her line of vision.

Nico rose and Andy took his place behind the desk.

Andy told her in a cold voice that she could come down to the police station to have a formal statement taken, or she could make her formal statement right here and now in front of witnesses.

He read her legal rights under the law, anything she said would be used in evidence against her. She had the right to have a legal representative with her.

She waived that right.

She knew it was stupid.

AN AFFAIR TO REMEMBER

But she was innocent.

Elena lifted her chin, and so it began.

Three endless hours later, Elena's head was banging and her eyes were hard and dry.

But it was the hard rock of solid ice in her heart that kept her going.

Not once did she falter.

Not once did her evidence deviate from anything but the truth.

And not once did the man she loved say one word in her defence.

Not once.

Her hand was perfectly steady now when she read through her statement and signed it.

"You can go now, Miss. Kennedy. There are further investigations taking place. Please leave your personal cell phone with my sergeant and your personal laptop."

"The laptop is at home, the cottage." She lifted her purse, took out her keys and tossed them on the desk. "Feel free to go through the house, take anything you need."

She wouldn't be going back to the cottage.

Ever.

All Elena could think was that she'd gone from having everything to having nothing.

The sense of injustice was so overwhelming, the anger that burned bright and burned hot in her belly, all of it, almost floored her. But no one would ever guess just by looking at her that her world had ended.

She wouldn't give them the fucking satisfaction.

How dare they sit there in judgement of her?

Nico Ferranti hadn't once taken his eyes from her.

She knew his reputation, the man made a bad enemy.

Well, wake up and smell the roses, pal, because Elena Margaret Mary Kennedy made an even worse enemy. And as for Marc Atelier? Well he could fuck off, too. So much for the love of his life. Yeah right. As soon as bad times happened, he'd lined up against her. Oh, they might have email *evidence*. But Elena wasn't stupid. They'd have a hell of a time proving *she* was the person who sent those emails. Everyone used her office during the working day. The office was a hub. Anyone could have used her email. Her mind now flew over the people who had access. The list wasn't a particularly long one. But she'd put good money on it that none of them, not one, would do something like this.

Yeah right.

The truth was the truth, one of the people she worked with every single day, people she admired, people she respected, one of them had set her up.

Fucking coward.

The police were leaving, the security team, too.

Now there was only Nico, Julie and a beyond furious Elena in the room.

"You are suspended with immediate effect on full pay until we get to the bottom of this, Miss Kennedy."

Miss Kennedy?

When the hell had Nico ever called her Miss Kennedy.

Julie rose, placed a hand on her shoulder and pressed.

"I'll get your coat and your things, you can go out the French doors to your car."

Saving her the walk of shame?

The small act of kindness by Julie almost broke Elena, but she rose to her feet.

Her car keys were attached to her house keys.

Elena slipped her car keys from the keychain and dropped the keys onto Nico's desk.

The pride of a long line of Celts who'd fought injustice through generations now hardened her heart, her head.

Her chin jerked high as she looked down her nose at Nico Ferranti, a man she'd trusted, a man she'd admired.

"Eventually, you will realise that you've made a big mistake today, Nico. I'm innocent. Before I was marched in here a full investigation should have taken place to ascertain exactly who had access to my computer on those days."

He opened his mouth to respond, but Elena held up her hand.

"There is nothing you can say to me either now or in the future when you learn the truth, that will make up for the harm you have done to me this day. Nothing. I can promise you one thing, however. I will never, ever, set foot inside this building again. Loyalty is not a one way street, Mr. Ferranti, it flows both ways. Please have my belongings forwarded to my father's address. I will only correspond with you via my lawyers."

Julie returned with her coat and Elena thanked her politely as she shrugged it on and buttoned it right up to the neck. It almost felt as if she was putting on armour to ready herself for the battle ahead. And by God she was going to give the whole rotten lot of them a battle they'd never forget.

Elena picked up her purse, her car keys and moved with Julie to the French doors. She was sneaking out like a thief in the night. And she'd never forgive the person who'd brought her down like this, or the rest of them for not trusting her, either.

But before she left, she turned to Nico and a white-faced Julie.

"Oh, and you can tell Marc Atelier that he's had his fun. It's finished."

Elena slammed the door behind her.

Head held high, she marched to her car.

Nico held up his hand as Julie went to speak, he picked up a pen, wrote on a note and handed it to her.

The room is bugged.

Julie's eyes went wide before she nodded her head.

Then she scribbled on her pad.

What the hell is going on?

Nico shook his head.

"If you could arrange for Miss. Kennedy's belongings to be boxed and sent to her, please Julie?"

Her eyes held his before she nodded.

"Certainly, sir."

Chapter Fifteen

As Elena drove away from Ludlow Hall, dusk was falling fast and the temperature right along with it. She was numb. Knuckles white, her hands clung to the steering wheel of her red mini cooper. She couldn't feel her fingers, couldn't feel her feet.

After university, where she'd studied marketing and communications, and a lonely spell in London working for a multi-national finance company, the recession had struck and she'd headed back to the place she knew well. She'd always known she'd move back to the vibrant market town of Old Ludlow. The Kennedy's went back four generations. Elena wanted her future children, if she had any, to have a repeat of her rock solid and respectable childhood - making lifelong friends from kindergarten right through to college; knowing all the people from church; the town hall; the brownies; the guides; the skating club; the riding club; and everything that underpinned the whole, family.

And it was to family she headed now.

Not so long ago, she'd imagined moving back to town with her own family, with an adoring husband and a couple of kids. But life hadn't worked out like that. She'd never met the man who made her tingles tingle.

Until a week ago.

Just thinking about Marc brought a scorching lump to her throat.

When the ice in her heart threatened to melt, she growled like a she-wolf and it froze right back up again.

As Elena drove through the high street of Old Ludlow, she didn't see the Christmas lights in the shape of big stars strung high over the road. She didn't see trees, stripped of leaves, their branches strung with thousands of fairy lights. She didn't see the last minute shoppers, weighed down with gifts.

All she saw was home.

AN AFFAIR TO REMEMBER

As she drove out of town and the car rose up the hill, she saw the Kennedy house, as it was known by the locals, sitting proud and alone backed by a pine forest and skirted at the front by her father's pride and joy, a smooth lawn, covered in snow. Her car climbed the private road, up, up until it levelled off to a large turning circle with a huge coniferous tree in the centre. Her brothers, as they did every year, had covered the tree in thousands of twinkling fairy lights. The house itself had been constructed in a red brick during the reign of Queen Victoria, three stories with may steep gables. The ground floor had rows of bay windows with white shutters. Someone had left the kitchen and porch lights on. Eyes swimming now, Elena rummaged around for the door key and realised it was still on the keychain she'd left in Nico's office at Ludlow Hall.

Damn it.

She sniffed as tears poured down her face.

But she would not be broken.

Next to the front door she saw the plant pot filled with happy pansies and remembered the secret hiding place for the spare key. That's if the key was still there because the men who lived in the house weren't known for putting things back where they belonged.

She climbed out of the car and was immediately slapped by an icy wind.

Freezing fingers tipped back the rock next to the flower pot and there was the key. She closed her eyes and thanked God. Her fingers were so cold it took two attempts to get the key in the lock and open the door. And immediately the warmth and smell of home took her in its loving arms and hugged her tight.

The sound of scrabbling paws on the oak floor and a loud woof had her brace herself against the door.

"Hey, baby."

And here he came, her darling boy, eighty pounds of unconditional love, a shaggy coat, a crazy tail and a loving tongue. His paws were on her shoulders as he yipped in doggy delight then he dropped and rolled to lay on his back dark eyes dancing, his pink tongue lolling just begging for his belly to be rubbed.

"Hello Czar, darling. Who's a good boy? Who's my bestest boy?"

Czar was a German Shepherd which belonged to Liam and was an ex-police dog who'd been injured in the line of duty, stabbed, and medically retired from the force. Czar ruled the roost over the Kennedy clan.

Elena slumped to the floor, and since this was not normal behaviour for the youngest member of the Kennedy's, Czar dropped on his butt, cocked his head and looked at her as if to say, "What's the matter, darling?"

And Elena promptly burst into tears.

Well, Czar wasn't having that, not on his watch.

So he did his best to sit on her lap and lick the tears away.

By the time he was finished Elena was crying with laughter and crying with heartbreak and crying because she was so very glad to be home safe and sound.

And that was how retired Police sergeant Daniel Kennedy found his baby girl.

Elena lifted her head from Czar's fur, mascara running her down her cheeks.

Her chin wobbled.

"Hi, Daddy."

Three hours later, Elena was sprawled on a huge sofa in the family room, the focus of which was an enormous stone fireplace big enough to roast a cow. She was wrapped in a lambs' wool blanket in a tartan designed and woven for the House Of Bruar in Scotland. Her eyes were so swollen from a crying jag that her father patted her head and told her not to worry because everything would look much better in the morning.

Since parts of the house were freezing, she was dressed in two pairs of ancient sweat pants and a variety of layers topped with one of her brother's sweatshirts. And she had three pairs of thick socks on her feet.

Daniel Kennedy had the colouring and the cheekbones of the black Irish. Meaning his hair, although going grey at the sides, was black as jet. As were his bushy brows. His eyes were a rich brown and his skin was olive, stretched tight across razor sharp cheekbones. He was six foot five inches in his bare feet, one hundred and eighty pounds and, in the words of the widow Mrs. Johnston who manned the farm shop, a fine figure of a man. Her dad placed a cup of hot chocolate in her hands, pressed his mouth to the top of her head and made himself comfortable in a fat chair.

"Liam and Adam are bringing pizza with all the trimmings, beer and wine, Ben and Jerry's Boston Cream Pie, and chocolate," he told her in a gruff voice. A voice he saved for the rare occasion when he found dealing with his baby girl when she was sad a little... overwhelming.

"Thanks, Dad," Elena said and sniffed pathetically. "I'm just finding the whole thing really... intense."

"Uh huh."

Her eyes meet her father's and all she could see was unconditional love and support.

Unconditional.

And just like that her eyes pooled again.

Czar whined from the floor where he lay at her feet.

The dog hadn't left her side since she'd arrived, even when she'd had a nice hot bath he'd stood guard over her, just in case she was sucked down the drain with the bath water and he might need to jump in and save her. Crazy dog. The only thing he was scared of was the sound of water draining away after the bath plug was pulled.

The sound of cars roaring up the drive way had Czar leap to his feet and trot out the door, tail high, to repel all boarders. Of course he recognised the sound of the engines and the sound of banging doors, the loud male voices. In this house everyone yelled. It was the only way to get a word in.

Elena heard the sounds of home, the clatter of boots being dumped, someone wrestling the dog and then the sitting room door flew open.

"So, what the hell's happening with my baby sister?" Liam yelled as he walked through the door.

Dressed in jeans and a short-sleeved T-shirt, which used to be black but had been washed to many shades of grey, that showcased rock hard abs and amazing guns. It appeared her brothers were not like other mortals, because the Kennedy boys were immune to temperatures below freezing. Liam dumped four boxes of extra large pizza on the table and tossed a thick bundle of paper napkins on top. Adam followed right behind, dressed in a similar uniform, except his T-shirt told the world that he was sexy, baby, which was nothing but the truth. Adam placed an open bottle of Pinot Grigio, a wine glass and a pack of six beers on the coffee table.

They might drive her crazy at times, but Elena could not deny the men in her family were hawt. Every single one of her brothers had the Kennedy colouring, dark. Liam was a member of the regional police SWAT team. Adam was part of something else called the police Rapid Reaction Force. Basically both were good with guns. And like all the Kennedy men, they struggled to fight women off with tear gas and water cannon.

"Apparently, I sell intimate details of Nico's personal life to a trashy tabloid. I've been suspended from work. And I've given a statement to your illustrious leader, Chief Inspector Bradshaw," Elena told Liam. "Why don't you ask him what's happening?"

"Oooooooh, bitchy," Liam sang.

"Liam," Daniel warned.

Elena turned big eyes filled with pretend hurt on her father.

"Why did you give me brothers, Dad? Couldn't you have tried harder for girls? Just think, instead of Liam you might have had a Leona."

Daniel winked at her and smiled proudly.

Adam, who was the spitting image of their father, lifted Elena's feet, sat down and placed them on his lap. He turned twinkling dark eyes on her and rubbed her toes with his big strong fingers.

"You look like shit," he told her in a tone filled to the brim with brotherly solidarity. "Your face is all swollen and blotchy and your nose is red. Hasn't Andy phoned you?"

Gotta love brothers, they tell a girl just the way it is and never pretty up the truth.

"They took my cell phone and my laptop. Ergo, Einstein, I don't have any means of communication."

"Is that *my* sweatshirt you're wearing?" Liam demanded, his beer stalled half way to his mouth as he eyed her clothes.

"I'm in the middle of a nervous breakdown, pal. It was an emergency."

He pointed a finger. "Make sure I get it back washed and ironed."

"Dad," Adam said as he scrolled through his cell. "Did Andy call home?"

"You mean like, E.T?" Liam cackled, cracking himself up.

Liam was getting on her nerves.

And why wasn't he taking her situation seriously?

"Nope," her father said, a man of few words.

But one thing was bothering Elena now.

She was in the middle of a crisis.

A crisis of epic proportions.

So why weren't the men in her family treating her mental breakdown with the respect it deserved?

Adam was ignoring the way her foot was jabbing him in the ribs and instead listening with rapt attention to a message on his cell.

He tossed the phone on the table, grabbed a pizza box, opened the lid and offered Elena first dibs. His way of saying, 'Don't worry, darling.'

She chose a slice of pepperoni and then thanked Liam for plucking the mug of hot chocolate out of her hand and replacing it with a glass of wine. His response to her mumble of thanks was to rub his knuckles on her skull, which meant her brother loved her more than life.

She took a healthy gulp of wine, chewed on her pie and stared miserably into the fire.

How could a woman be on top of the world one minute and then dropped into the fires of hell the next minute?

Where on earth had it all gone wrong?

Elena sniffed as a single tear pooled and tipped over.

And she didn't notice three grown men staring at her with an *Aww*, look in their eyes.

Czar was one of those rare animals, a dog who didn't beg for food at the table. From his prone position in front of the fire, his ears twitched and then his head rose before he got to his feet and did his doggie trot, tail held high, as he moved out the room and down the corridor to the door.

His single woof coincided with the sound of a car door closing.

Probably her brother Joe. He was a doctor. A man who was good in a family emergency. And a man who could dispense drugs. Elena knew she could do with something to knock her out cold. Oblivion sounded like a great place to visit for a while.

The doorbell rang.

And in the way of families where everyone and their friends came and went without knocking or ringing the bell, they all went utterly still.

Daniel looked at Elena.

Elena looked at Adam.

Adam looked at Liam.

Nobody moved.

After an exaggerated eye roll, Liam put down his beer, his slice of pizza, and got up to answer the door.

The sound of male voices made Elena's ears prick.

Maybe it was the police?

But then she heard a voice she knew well tell Czar he was big beautiful beast.

Shitty shit shit.

Elena placed her wine, her pizza on the table and dived under the blankets with a panicked,

"Tell him I'm not here."

So she missed the way her father's brow flew into his hairline and the way Adam grinned like a Cheshire cat.

"Sure, come on in," Liam said, to the person Elena did not want to see, as he entered the sitting room with the unwelcome guest. "She's right here on the sofa. What the hell are you doing under there, Elena? You've gotta visitor."

Under the blanket Elena's heart was acting crazy in her chest, drumming a beat like Virgil Donati on crack, in other words, too fast.

Silence.

"Elena?" Marc said.

"FUCK OFF!" she yelled.

Cue another long and collectively stunned silence.

Still under the blanket, Elena made a face and squeezed her eyes shut, because she'd never, ever, in her whole life, EVER cursed in the house of her father.

"You're going to get a spanking for that," Marc said.

Chapter Sixteen

"Right, son," Daniel Kennedy, said into the second stunned silence in as many minutes. "We'll leave you two to it."

"Thank you, sir," growled Marc.

Sir?

Creep.

Sucking up to her father like that.

Hiding under a blanket like this was quite a ridiculous situation to be in, Elena realised, and wondered if she was seriously losing her tiny mind.

She might be behaving like it, but she wasn't five years old.

She was an adult.

But before she could do anything, the cover was pulled back to reveal an angry Marc Atelier glaring down at her. Very angry.

Elena could tell by the way his blue eyes drilled into hers, by the way his hair was a mess, as if he'd been running his hands through it. And by the way his strong jaw was clenched too tight. He was dressed in jeans tucked into black boots, a gorgeous black sweater and a grey puffa jacket.

He looked... gorgeous.

But Elena turned her head to stare into the fire, she didn't want him here, or in her life.

She wanted him gone.

"Get out," she said.

The response was a low throaty growl before she was hauled to her feet and shaken until her teeth rattled.

"What the *hell* is the matter with you?" he roared.

She blinked up into his furious face.

And just like that her temper roared like a lion.

"Excuse me? Who was the one who just stood there while I was grilled for hours?HOURS!" she yelled right back at him. "Not once did you defend me. How could you just stand there like that? You simply tossed me to the wolves and stepped back."

He released her so fast she stumbled.

Then he paced to the fire and back.

Now he stood in front of her, in her personal space, hands on hips and jutted his chin.

"I'm not talking about all that crap. I'm talking about you telling Nico that you've finished with me. Are you fucking crazy?"

Crap?

What had happened to her today wasn't crap. It was so far removed from crap that...

Wait a minute.

Mind spinning, Elena sank to the couch, took a gulp of wine.

She didn't offer him a drink because as far as she was concerned he'd arrived uninvited and wasn't welcome.

"Explain the crap comment to me."

Marc heaved a deeply frustrated sigh of a male at the end of his tether.

Without asking he took a bottle beer from the pack, unscrewed the top and drank deeply.

"If you had just waited in Nico's office for a few more minutes, you would have realised that you were in the clear."

The room spun and Marc's face seemed to zoom out and then zoom back into focus.

In the clear?

"But... you never said a single word. You just stood there while they grilled me. At any moment I was expecting water boarding or electric cattle prods."

"Now you're being ridiculous," he said.

Obviously not fearing for his life he used a tone that pressed a hot button, a red haze misted before her eyes.

"It was the worst afternoon of my entire life," she yelled at the top of her voice.

Unlike Tom, Marc remained unfazed by an angry woman.

He shook his head.

Now his eyes stayed on hers.

"You handled them like a pro. I was so terribly proud of you. You stood your ground. Baby, you were amazing."

Elena blinked frantically as the red haze evaporated.

Her emotions felt as if they were on an elastic band being bounced all over the place.

Then those magic words he'd uttered earlier flew into her confused brain.

"I'm in the clear?"

"Yes. It was Jenny."

Elena couldn't tear her eyes from his and saw the truth.

"Jenny? *My* Jenny? Lovely little Jenny who's been doing a wonderful job? I just can't believe it."

Now Marc came to sit next to her and threw his arm around her shoulder.

"Yeah, well. It's a long story. Let's get your dad and brothers in here so I only have to tell it once."

"Okay."

Elena couldn't say that she felt that all was right with her world now she was in the clear, because it wasn't, but she did feel as if a huge weight had been lifted from her shoulders.

She turned to look up into Marc's face, saw him studying hers carefully.

"Oh baby, you've been crying for nothing. Once we'd finished with Jenny, I rushed to find you. And you'd gone. Nico's frantic. And you left your cell phone behind."

Now her eyes narrowed into his.

"If you remember, I was instructed to hand my cell phone to the police."

"Point taken." He stood. "I'll get your dad and brothers."

He didn't have to go far because they were standing right outside the door.

And every single one looked... pissed.

"Come in," Marc said.

They did and took their positions.

Liam lifted Elena and dropped her between him and Adam on the sofa, and her father sat in his chair.

AN AFFAIR TO REMEMBER

Marc had faced the Taliban and Al Qaeda insurgents and never felt the lick of fear up his spine he was feeling now.

Man, the Kennedy's were big bastards.

All three men had folded their muscled arms.

And all three were giving him the stink eye.

He focused on Elena.

Poor baby.

She'd had a helluva day, but he'd only spoken the truth. She'd been amazing. Not once had she faltered when speaking to Nico or Andy Bradshaw. He knew she'd been shaking inside, and no wonder. But not once had she shown anything except a stiff pride laced with plenty of courage.

A courage that made him proud.

He paced to the fire and back, glanced at the dog who looked as if it was laughing at him.

Yeah, well, there was nothing funny about all this.

Nothing funny at all.

Marc took a breath.

"Right. So... Nico called me in to Ludlow Hall from my base at The Ferranti Hotel and Spa at Lake Como in Italy. It's a handy central hub for Europe."

"You live in Italy?" Elena piped up.

"Well, yeah. I mean, I did. I don't now because I need to be back in England for my mum and my sister. My dad passed away four months ago," Marc said to Elena's father who was watching him closely.

"Sorry for your loss," Daniel growled. "Family is everything."

Marc stared at him.

"Yes. Yes, it is. Anyway. Nico called me and my team in because information was being leaked to a tabloid. Little trickles that on their own might not mean much, but put together were very damaging to Nico and his family..."

"I couldn't believe the things in those emails. I felt sick to my stomach when I read them," Elena said.

"Yeah. Well, not everything was used by the journalist, but she used enough."

"What journalist?" Adam piped up.

"Um. Tabitha Crew. Anyway, we set up an investigation, checking all email traffic and company cell phone traffic from Ludlow Hall. And we narrowed the mole down to housekeeping, reception, and the administration staff. And then we found the majority of the messages embedded in Elena's email account."

"So, was our relationship based on a lie? Did you sleep with me to see if I was the one selling secrets?"

He blinked and stared at her as if she was talking in tongues.

All three men, and the dog, sat up tall and straight as if a red hot poker had been stuck up their ass.

And by the *way* they were looking at him.

Dear Christ.

He was a dead man.

"No! No! We didn't find your connection until yesterday. But I knew there was no way you'd do such a thing. It was a poor attempt by someone to cover their tracks."

She didn't look convinced.

More importantly neither did her father and two brothers.

All three had their eyes lasered on him.

Bloody hell.

Marc shoved his hands through his hair and battled on.

"Anyway. We found two bugs in Nico's office..."

"Bugs?"

"Recording devices," Adam told Elena then nodded for Marc to continue.

"It's all very James Bond," she spoke her thoughts out loud.

Marc just stared hard at her.

"Riiiight. But we also knew we needed to flush out the mole. We knew it wasn't you, but we'd narrowed it down to the reception team. We looked very closely at family members, partners. And we found that Jenny's boyfriend works for the same tabloid as Tabitha Crew. So we knew we had her," Marc said.

He looked Elena dead in the eye.

"And that's where you came in. Jenny adores you. If she thought you were in deep trouble, we figured she'd break. And sure enough when we got the reception staff all together to tell them that you'd been suspended, Jenny burst into tears. It took a couple of hours to get her statement straight. She wanted her mother. And it all took time."

"You set me up," Elena whispered, her eyes filled with a hurt that caught his lungs.

Marc's throat went dry.

He looked at her brothers, her father, for help.

But none was to be found.

"No. Yes. Well... not really. You would still have been questioned by the police. That's standard procedure. The reason we did it in Nico's office, with a formal caution was..."

"You cautioned my sister?" Liam said in a soft voice.

Marc frowned, cleared his dry throat.

He was in deep doo doo.

When he'd laid the plan out to Nico, the pair of them had admired the straightforward beauty of his concept. After a couple of glasses of bubbly, the idea had seemed so simple and straightforward. In his mind, he had, to be honest, sort of skated over Elena's part in the plan, believing that she'd be tough enough to handle whatever was thrown at her.

Now he could see the fatal flaw in his thinking.

Now he was wondering what the *hell* he'd been thinking?

He'd hurt her.

Scared her.

He was an idiot.

Desperately, Marc attempted to climb out the deep hole he'd dug for himself.

"As I said, cautioning a witness who is a suspect in a criminal offence, is standard procedure in a case like this. But the main reason we did it was for the benefit of the person listening. We'd left the recording devices where they were. It was imperative that whoever was listening believed that you were genuinely in trouble."

Now Elena stood and Marc could see she was furious.

Her family looked as if they could chew nails.

Shit.

"You set me up. Have you any idea what I went through this afternoon? Have you?"

She was shaking, her hazel eyes all teary.

Fuck.

"I knew you were innocent and Nico wanted action, fast. This way your name is cleared and we have the culprit. Job done."

"Job done?" she repeated.

Marc held up his hands and had a bad feeling things were going from bad to worse.

"You still have your job. As soon as Nico knew you were in the clear he raced back to his office, but you'd gone. He even chased your car down the car park. He's pretty messed up about the whole thing."

Now her brows rose.

And Marc realised that Elena was not listening to him, not really.

"He deserves to be messed up. I told Nico Ferranti that I knew I'd be cleared. I also told him that I'd never set foot in his hotel again. He can stuff his job. I want to work for someone I can trust. I want to have a man standing by my side through thick and thin, through the bad times and the good."

Now Marc frowned because he knew the man she was talking about was him.

"I am standing by you. Why won't you listen to me?"

"You call standing by me setting me up for some sort of sting? Couldn't you have told me *why* you were at Ludlow Hall in the first place?"

Marc shook his head.

She didn't understand.

No. She didn't want to understand, he realised now.

He got that she'd been through a horrible ordeal.

Of course he did.

But he'd had a job to do.

And he'd done it.

They'd caught the bad guys.

It was time to move on.

AN AFFAIR TO REMEMBER

He felt sick because he had a question to ask her and he could already see the answer in her eyes.

"What about us?"

Her eyes went colder than ice.

"There is no us."

Chapter Seventeen

Every year, Elena cooked Christmas dinner, with all the trimmings, for her family and a couple of close friends who'd otherwise spend the day alone.

The preparations started on Christmas Eve in an attempt to ensure the day itself went off without a hitch. She didn't see the hard work as a chore. And under normal circumstances, she loved the whole festive vibe. But this year all she wanted to do was curl up in a dark room, throw the comforter over her head and forget about it.

She was standing at the kitchen sink scrubbing a mountain of potatoes, the mindless task was actually therapeutic. Her dad was sitting at the kitchen table peeling carrots, while four of her six brothers were *helping* by drinking beer and goofing around. The two brothers missing were overseas, training foreign fighters to defend their land.

Last night she'd slept like a log.

Which had come as a pleasant surprise, since her body was aching for Marc. Who knew heartache actually ached? It hurt. She could even press the spot between her ribs where it hurt. Nico had phoned the house, twice, to speak to her, but she refused to take his calls. Eventually, her father had told him to leave his daughter in peace, that she'd been through enough. Even the Chief Inspector of police, Andy Bradshaw, had called in Liam and Adam and explained he'd only been doing his duty. Her brothers appreciated it, agreed with him and understood. But they were standing by their sister. Elena had been shaken up pretty badly. She needed time to assimilate everything that had happened to her. That's what family did, they stuck together through everything. They had each other's backs. The trouble was nobody at Ludlow Hall had her back that day. Not even the man who was supposed to love her, and Elena would never forget it, or forgive it.

AN AFFAIR TO REMEMBER

She was suffering, a little voice told her, with a bad case of the Kennedy stubbornness gene. Actually, Elena responded. It was more like Karma. People get back what they put out there, so Nico and Marc and Andy could just suck it up.

Earlier in the day, she'd gone out for a long walk with Czar, like the good dog he was, loping along off the leash at her heel. And during that walk she'd taken time-out for herself, from the Christmas chaos of the family home, to just... think.

Her affair with Marc had burned incredibly hot, maybe too hot. And fast, maybe too fast. They'd made promises to each other without really knowing the other. Without really thinking things through. So when they hit a bump in the road (more like an earthquake) they had nowhere soft to land.

But the part that really left a bitter taste in her mouth, was the part where he'd come up with a plan to set her up without warning. How could he do such a thing, stand there, let them tear her to pieces for hours and say nothing? She just couldn't get her head around it. But then she remembered that the room had been bugged. She sniffed, it was all so confusing.

A strong arm was slung around her shoulder.

"Elena, you've scrubbed that potato for ten minutes," Joe said.

She turned to look up into his tired face, even tired her favourite brother was handsome.

Joe had the unenviable task of being a resident doctor in Accident and Emergency. Just like his brothers in the army and the police, he manned the front line in a hospital system that was strapped for cash. And Joe was exhausted.

"How much sleep did you get last night?"

"Four hours. Luxury."

"Why don't you take a nap?"

"Nah. I'm used to it. If I go to bed now I'll be prowling the house at four a.m. and driving everybody nuts. Why don't we go out for a walk into town? I'll even spring for a drink at the pub. It might make both of us feel better."

Sounded like a plan.

Elena didn't tell him she'd already walked miles this morning, she valued any time she had with Joe. He was the second eldest, the voice of reason and a good listener.

Ten minutes later, Joe and Elena were wrapped up in layers under duck-down puffa jackets with ski hats pulled down low and yards of woollen scarves wound around their neck. Czar was playing hide and seek in the snow drifts at the side of the road as they strolled down the lane.

"So, what's this I hear about you and Marc Atelier? Sounds complicated. Is it serious?"

"I thought it was serious," Elena said. She added a heavy sigh and tucked her arm in his. "We just clicked, you know? I thought, at last, I've found the one for me."

Her big brother stopped to look into her eyes.

"Do you love him?"

Did she?

"We had the most amazing weekend together. And for most of this week, and even at work, it was good, you know? We ate, cooked together, slept together. It was right."

"Do you love him?"

When she didn't respond Joe's brows rose.

She couldn't lie to him.

So she shouldn't lie to herself.

"Yes, I love him. I can't stop." Now Elena spun around to kick a snow drift. Czar pounced on the clump of snow like a cat on a mouse. "He's made me so mad, Joe. I just want to punch him. He hurt me and I don't know if I can get past it."

Joe pulled her into him, slung his arm around her shoulders and they continued to walk into the town, heading for an ancient tavern that had been serving travellers for four hundred years called The Bull's Head.

"You need a drink."

Joe shoved open the pub door, whistled for Czar who came to heel. Elena clipped on his leash and found a table in the corner while Joe went to the bar to order drinks. She pulled off her hat, her gloves and her scarf and unzipped her coat. There was a fire roaring in the grate and the place was crammed with revellers. Elvis was crooning something about a blue Christmas without you. The lyrics seemed to make the ache in her heart more intense.

Joe pushed back through the crowd doing a juggling act with a glass of white wine and a pint of beer. He nodded to neighbours and acquaintances, and returned insults in the spirit to which they'd been given to his pals. He placed the glass of white wine in front of Elena and took a sip of his pint. He straddled a stool and tugged off his hat and scarf, handed them to Elena who had space in her little nook to stash their stuff. Czar flopped to the floor under the table, eyes closed, ears on alert for incoming like radar.

"Cheers," Joe said and they clinked glasses. Her brother's dark eyes searched her face. "I think you should consider looking at what happened from Marc's point of view. Haven't you been reading what's been printed in the press about the Ferranti's?"

Elena shook her head.

"I lead a very busy life. I don't have time to read trashy gossip."

"Yeah, well, maybe you should make time. After all you work at Ludlow Hall and Nico's your boss. Knowledge is power. Some of the stuff was nasty. Rumours about affairs and rumours that the marriage was in trouble."

"That's utter nonsense," Elena said.

"Yeah, well, not everyone believes it's lies. The couple have been having a really hard time. Even to me, it appears as if someone's got it in for Nico. There was stuff in the financial press, too, about something in Italy. For a few months it looked as if he was in big trouble. But then that petered out, too. Marc works for Nico as a security expert. I'm betting Marc keeps a close eye on nefarious stuff and nips things in the bud all the time. I bet that's why he was based in Italy, too."

"You make him sound like James Bond."

Joe grinned. He was a big fan of the film franchise.

"Apart from you and me, kiddo, we're a family of police and military men. Liam and Adam like Marc, a lot. They recognise one of their own. And they did a little digging. The guy's a hero. He had a very hard start in life and rose above it."

111

When Elena frowned into wine, Joe studied her face carefully.

"He didn't tell you about his past?"

She shook her head.

"Only that he was adopted and the people who took him took his half-sister, too, when she was a baby. He loves his adopted mother very much. And you're right, he is close to Nico."

"Think about it. He's ex-military, ex-police. What you felt was a hot grilling, a grilling that made you crap your panties, he'd regard as no big deal. And from what I could tell he thought you were a star. He's really proud of you, babe. But then you're a Kennedy. I'd expect nothing less."

"He set me up for his own ends."

"He did it to stop the leak." He waited a couple of beats. "You like Bronte?"

"Of course I like Bronte."

"Thanks to you, Bronte's going to stop being hurt by a vicious tabloid bitch. Bronte loves Nico. Nico loves Bronte. Nico hurts, Bronte hurts."

Elena took time to mull his words over in her mind.

By this time they'd finished their drinks.

They started to pile on their jackets and hats and scarves and gloves.

As they pushed through the crowd with Czar, Elena knew she had a great deal to think about.

Joe stamped his feet as fresh snow started to fall.

"All I'm saying is that maybe you should give the guy a chance. It's the season of goodwill. Think about it."

He slung his arm around her and she wound her arm around his waist.

"Love sucks," she muttered.

"Tell me about it. Loving someone isn't always a personal choice. Count yourself lucky you've fallen for one of the good guys. Nothing worse than being in love with the wrong person. Now that is hell."

Elena looked up into his face, but Joe was looking straight ahead, his mouth firm.

Her brother looked... sad.

She was dying to ask him what was wrong.

But Joe was a very private person, a deep thinker, and she knew better than to open old hurts, old wounds best left alone.

She pulled him tight into her side as they trudged up the hill to their home, both deep in thought.

Elena was still deep in thought as she prepared stuffing for the turkey.

The ring of the doorbell had everyone look at each other in the kitchen.

No one moved until Liam muttered something intelligible and moved down the hallway to open the door.

"Hey, gorgeous. What can I do for you?"

"Can I speak to Elena?"

"Sure, come on in."

Bronte Ferranti stepped into the kitchen. Her coat was taken as she was hugged and kissed by a long line of men, including Elena's father.

By the time they'd finished, her face was flushed and her green eyes were sparkling with suppressed laughter.

"Sorry to interrupt, I know it's a busy time for everyone." Her eyes found Elena's. The laughter slid away. Bronte bit her lip. "Can I talk to you for a minute?"

Well, the Ferranti's had really brought out the big guns if Bronte was standing in her father's kitchen.

"Come on through to the sitting room. Would you like a drink?"

Elena led the way.

Nico's blonde wife shook her head.

"No, thank you. I've left Nico home alone with the kids. Trust me, it's a recipe for disaster, especially the night before Christmas. The twins are bouncing off the walls."

The girls moved through the hall and into the sitting room with its battered old couch and mismatched chairs. The space was filled with the detritus of family life. Newspapers, magazines, dirty mugs and plates and tennis shoes.

Elena's face burned.

She was going to kill her brothers.

They lived like pigs.

"Sorry about the mess. I only clean in here about five times a day."

"Please, don't worry about it. You have a lovely home. I've always thought so. Look, first of all I just want to say that the men in our lives were completely out of order to put you in the middle of this big mess."

Elena blinked.

But before she could speak, Bronte carried on.

"It's so *typical* of Nico to just power over people and their feelings. He's so overprotective of me and the kids. You'd think I was a shrinking violet or something. He's going to apologise to you, Elena. All I'm asking is that you hear him out. He's devastated that he's hurt you. He's even more upset that he's lost you from The Hall. But it's his own fault."

"Well, they did find those emails on my PC. He had to question me. I understand that and I accept it. It was just the way it was done, Bronte. I've never been so scared in my life. And Marc wouldn't even look at me..."

"Stupid. They're stupid, Elena. Marc's looking as if he's lost his best friend. His mother's arrived, and his sister, and they're worried sick about him. As if the poor things haven't been through enough with losing John so suddenly. Marc's moved into Heron's Rest so they can all be together. And he's planning that they stay for a while, to give his mother a chance to find her feet again. Poor woman. They were married for over forty years you know. So it's been very hard on everyone."

Elena felt awful, just awful, that Marc's mother was suffering such heartbreak.

Bronte turned big emerald eyes on her and took her hands in hers and held on tight.

"Anyway. The reason I'm here is to try to build bridges. You can torture Nico for as long as you like, God knows the big lug deserves it. But, Elena, Marc is crazy about you. He doesn't know I'm here. He'd be furious. But I've known him for a number of years and even after John died he wasn't in this state. Please listen to what he has to say. Please give him a chance. We're having a little get together tonight at The Dower House. If you don't already have plans, please consider dropping by and bring all the family. It would be lovely for Mary and Nina to meet new people. Please, Elena."

What could she say against the force of nature that was Bronte Ferranti?

The woman's heartfelt plea would bring a tear to a glass eye.

Elena realised she had no choice.

"Okay," she said, making up her mind for the whole family. "We'll be happy to come. What time?"

"Seven-thirty. Oscar's prepared a buffet, so he'll be there with Emma. Trust me, you'll all have a great time. Bring the dog, too."

"That's very kind of you, but Czar will be fine on his own doing guard duty. What do I wear? Is it casual?"

"Jeans and a sweater. No big deal." Bronte hugged her tight. When she eased back her eyes were too bright. "Wonderful! I'll see you then. And thank you, Elena. Thank you so much."

Elena sat on the sofa for at least five minutes after Bronte left. Her eyes rose to check the time on the old carriage clock on the mantelpiece. Six-thirty, not a lot of time to organise five men. Nothing like a challenge.

She marched into the kitchen, grabbed a saucepan and banged a wooden spoon on the base. That got their attention. Immediately all the chat stopped as five males stared at her.

"We're off to The Dower House for a Christmas Eve get together to welcome a couple of new arrivals to our community. I'm in the shower first. You have exactly sixty minutes to get showered, shaved and changed. Starting now."

She raced out the door and up the stair and into one of the two family bathrooms before they could start moaning and groaning.

But at precisely seven-fifteen her brothers and her father were standing all present and correct at the bottom of the stair. And every one of them looked amazing. My God, her brothers, and father, certainly cleaned up well. It wasn't their usual custom, as a family, to venture out on Christmas Eve, except to church. Elena knew they were doing it for her and for Marc.

As the guys argued who was driving, they crammed into her dad's Land Rover Defender and left for The Dower House.

Elena let the voices roll over her head.

Her stomach was in knots and she felt physically sick.

She just hoped to hell she was doing the right thing.

Chapter Eighteen

The last thing Marc wanted to do was spend Christmas Eve socialising at The Dower House.

He hadn't heard a peep from Elena.

His second in command, Steve, told him he'd seen her in a pub in town with a tall, dark haired guy. Apparently they looked really cosy drinking wine and beer, with their heads close together, with eyes only for each other.

It hadn't taken her long to find someone else, Marc thought savagely as jealousy, a lousy emotion, had chewed up his gut and spat it out.

He'd showered, and on his mother's strict instructions, shaved.

Two pairs of anxious eyes had watched him like a couple of hawks all fucking day.

Waiting for him to burst into tears or something fucking stupid like that.

As if!

He clattered down the wide staircase of Heron's Rest to find his mother and sister all wrapped up warm and raring to go. Nina was looking her usual fabulous self. Her dark hair hung down her back. Bright blue eyes sparkled into his. She'd painted her full mouth pillar box red. The colour matched her sweater. Her slim legs were encased in black skinny jeans and flat over the knee suede boots. Her black duck down coat kept her nice and snug. She was growing up too damned fast. She'd be twenty-one next month. An adult. Where the hell had the time gone?

His mother looked cute, too, in her slim tunic sweater of cashmere the colour of pewter, smart black pants and ankle boots. She'd done something different with her hair. It made her look years younger. Her grey eyes were still haunted, but her smile was genuine as she rose on her tip toes to press a kiss to his cheek.

"We'd better get going or we'll be late," she said.

His mother had never been late for an appointment in her life.

But he didn't argue.

Instead he saw them safely to his SUV.

When they arrived at The Dower House, Marc hadn't been sure what to expect.

Maybe a crowd of neighbours and friends.

What he found, after Nico took their coats and welcomed his mother and sister to his home, were Elena, her brothers and her father, Oscar Kamani (the famous chef) and Emma Ludlow, Bronte's cousin.

And Nico and Bronte and the kids.

That was the sum total.

His heart was in his mouth at he took his mother to meet Elena, the woman who held his heart in his hands.

"Mum, I'd like you to meet Elena Kennedy."

Mary Jones took both of Elena's hands in hers and held on tight.

"Lovely to meet you at last. Are you ready to forgive my son?"

Elena met his eyes and held.

"Do you think he deserves forgiveness, Mrs. Jones?"

"Oh yes, dear. Just don't go too easy on him. Start as you mean to go on that's what I always say."

And thank you, Mother.

Before he could open his mouth, Bronte took their arms and guided them through the sitting room doors, into the hall and into a small room, a study.

"I come here when I need a few minutes to myself. Take as long as you like. I imagine you two have a lot to talk about."

And with that, she walked out and closed the door.

"She's a smooth operator," Elena said, as she strolled around the pretty room, fingered the novels, heavy on romance and thrillers, on the shelves.

She didn't look at him and Marc's heart fell.

AN AFFAIR TO REMEMBER

"I'm sorry I hurt you, Elena."

Now she turned to him, her gaze direct.

And once their eyes locked, he couldn't look away.

Taking it nice and easy, he moved into her to take her in his arms.

When she didn't push him away, he took it as a good sign.

She didn't touch him either.

Her chin had a stubborn edge to it as she leaned back to keep her eyes on his.

"You were just doing your job. I understand that now. It was a shame you had to flatten me to do it."

Not giving an inch.

Little devil.

He took her wrists, wound them around his neck and pulled her closer.

Soft breasts pressed against his chest and he could feel her heart beating fast, or was it his?

She smelled fabulous, flowers, shampoo and woman.

His woman.

"Do you want me on my knees, Elena? Is that what you want?"

Her eyes narrowed, but he didn't see any anger in them.

He didn't see any warmth either.

"It's a start. I was thinking more along the lines of you crawling on your hands and knees."

His brows rose as he took a chance and dropped a kiss on her nose.

She didn't blink.

"Forgive me?"

This time he pressed little kisses on her cheeks, her chin, at the side of her mouth.

"Is that the best you can do?" she murmured, watching his face through slitted eyes.

He smiled.

Her teeth sank into his chin.

And right there Marc knew that if she was taking bites out of him they were going to be okay.

"I love you. I've missed you so much."

Now his mouth was at her neck and he inhaled the scent of his woman.

"I missed you, too," she said and her arms came around his waist and held on tight.

"I'm sorry. I'm so sorry."

She eased back to look into his eyes and saw the strain around his mouth, around his eyes.

"Kiss me."

His smile lit up the room before he dipped his head and his mouth took hers.

His lips were cool and soft against hers. But Elena wanted more, so she took more. And he gave her everything she needed to heal a sore heart.

By the time they eased back they were both breathing heavily.

"We're guests," Elena said. "We'd better rejoin the party."

He took her hand before he opened the door to the sound of laughter and high voices that mingled with orchestral Christmas music.

"We'll have our own party later," he promised, as he tugged her down the hall.

"Marc..."

He stopped and turned to her face him.

"I still have the keys to the cottage. The log burner is on, the heating is on, the champagne is in the fridge. Your things are just where you left them."

"I always spend Christmas morning with my family," she said, not wanting to give too much, too soon.

"Me, too. Maybe we can get them together later in the day at Heron's Rest? But first I want you to myself tonight. I'm not waiting for you any longer, Elena." He placed a gentle kiss on her soft mouth. "Why don't you bring the food, the wine and we'll combine our turkeys? As my mother said, let's start as we mean to go on."

He moved to kiss her again when a voice interrupted.

"Elena. May I speak with you for a moment?"

120

She closed her eyes.

Nico.

"Give him a chance, baby," Marc whispered in her ear.

She nodded once.

Marc gave the hand he held to Nico and the Italian towed her into his study.

It appeared it was a night for studies.

This one was huge.

The antique desk was massive and there was a fire burning low in the grate behind an enclosed fire guard.

Nico shut the door, released her hand and moved to a low sofa made of butter soft leather the colour of mocha.

"Sit," he said.

She sat, looked into his face and lifted her chin in defiance.

His teeth tugged on his top lip.

"*Cara*, I am sorry that you had to go through the ordeal with the police, but..."

Elena held up her hand to stop another word.

"No buts. There's a formal disciplinary procedure for the company and you didn't follow it. I understand why you did it. But didn't it occur to you or James Bond out there that you might have recruited me? Don't you think that it sickened me to read what those emails said about you and Bronte?"

"*Si*, but I will do anything to protect *mia famiglia*."

Nico's grey eyes were stormy now.

And Elena saw the love, saw the fear for that love, too.

She nodded.

The man was just trying to protect the people who mattered most.

Elena got that.

"What's happened to Jenny?"

His brow rose.

"Do you really want to know?"

"Yes."

"She has been dismissed."

"That's it?"

"What more would you have me do?"

Good question.

"She's very young, Nico. It's easy to make mistakes when we're young. She's a very good worker, good with the clients. I believe her boyfriend was the bad influence and used her. Perhaps she deserves another chance?"

"Not working in my hotels."

Fair enough.

The man was tough on people who let him down.

She stood. "I accept your apology."

Nico rose and went to hug her.

But Elena shook her head.

Nico studied her face.

Now his smooth brow creased.

"You are not coming back to Ludlow Hall?"

"I haven't decided yet. But at the moment I'm leaning towards a fresh start somewhere new. So, you deserve another chance, but not Jenny? Double standards, Nico."

A whole stream of Italian invective poured from his mouth as Nico paced to his desk and back again to stand in front of her.

"You drive a hard bargain, Elena Kennedy. *Si*, she can have a role in my organisation. But not at Ludlow Hall. I will find a place for her in the new Boutique Hotel in London, under the watchful eye of a very tough, very experienced manager. One more slip and she is out."

"Okay, I'll come back," Elena agreed with a nod. Then her eyes met his. "And I want a raise, fifteen percent. I'm worth every penny."

For a stunned moment, Nico simply stared. His mouth twitched. He threw back his head and roared with laughter.

She was caught in a big hug and both cheeks kissed.

"Ah, *Bella, bella*. You will drive Marc *pazzo*. He is a lucky man."

"You didn't agree. I didn't hear the word yes."

"*Si*, you may have a raise, it is the least I can do." He grabbed her hand and headed for the door. "Come, let us join our families."

Chapter Nineteen

They dropped Marc's mother and sister at Heron's Rest, and then drove back to the cottage.

Marc took her hand, placed it on his thigh as he drove and she was happy to leave it there.

It was a beautiful night.

A clear night.

The sky twinkling with millions of stars and constellations.

As the car slowed, crunching through ice, to park before the cottage, he switched off the engine and turned to her.

"Our families blended well tonight. We're a good fit," he said.

He was right.

Her brothers had been merciless the way they'd teased the lovely Nina. The girl had been pink cheeked by the end of the night, her blue eyes, so like her brother's, dancing as she'd given as good as she got. And Marc's mother had got on with Elena's dad like a house on fire. Christmas was the time for family.

Now Elena turned to him and found Marc's eyes fixed on her face.

"Are we okay?" he wanted to know.

And the fact that he wasn't quite sure of her was a good thing, she decided.

However, Elena was, when she wasn't being stubborn, a fair-minded person, too.

"We're good."

He got out, jogged around the car to open her door.

Hand in hand they walked her up the path to the door of the cottage.

When she stepped into the hall, the scents of pine, Christmas and the wood burner told her she was home. Once their coats were hanging on the coat hooks, they padded into the sitting room and Elena stopped dead.

Someone had placed a real Christmas tree in front of the French windows. The six foot fir was decorated with gold and red baubles and hundreds of fairy lights.

"Like it?" he whispered in her ear.

Elena turned to him grinning from ear to ear.

"Did you do this?"

"It was a team effort. I carried it in and set it up. My mum and Nina did the decorating."

She wandered over to study the fragile glass baubles, some of them had tiny snow men and Santa's inside. They were gorgeous. Then she fell to her knees to check out the presents all beautifully wrapped in gold paper with red velvet ribbon under the tree. And her heart fell, Marc's presents were still at her family home.

She heard him pop a bottle of champagne and turned to him.

Her eyes went wide when she read the label on the bottle.

Nothing but the best, it cost a fortune.

"My presents to you are at home," she said.

With his eyes on hers, Marc strolled around the breakfast bar, placed the drinks on the coffee table, before joining her on the floor. His mouth took hers so fast her head spun. It spun even more when his tongue slipped in to dance with hers.

When he eased back her mouth was tingling, along with another part of her anatomy.

His hand reached out to pick up a small box wrapped in gold with a red velvet bow on the top. He rose and took her with him, towing her to the sofa, where he sat her on his knee.

He handed her the box.

"Open it."

Elena's heart was racing so fast against her ribs she was amazed he couldn't hear it.

Her eyes met his and she read an excitement clouded by anxiety.

Taking her time, she carefully removed the ribbon, placed it on the coffee table and then she peeled off the gold paper, placed it next to the ribbon. The black velvet box was square. Her eyes met his as she pressed the little gold button and the lid popped open. When her eyes saw the diamond, princess cut, set in a slim band of white gold, her eyes swam, even as her heart soared.

She couldn't speak.

Marc cleared his throat.

"Like it?"

She nodded.

"Marry me, Elena? Be a mother to my babies? Be my best friend? Be the love of my life?"

He took the box out of her nerveless fingers, removed the ring and placed it on the third finger of her left hand. It fit perfectly. She was blinking rapidly, trying to stop the flood of stupid tears pouring down her face. He caught her hands in his, brought them to his lips and kissed her fingers one by one. And all the while his eyes never left hers.

"Yes, I'll marry you. Have your babies. Be your best friend. I love you, so much, Marc."

They sealed the deal with a kiss.

*****

The afternoon of Christmas day found the Kennedy clan and their friends and the Jones family all sitting down at a vast table in the dining kitchen of Heron's Rest.

There was a lot of laughter, fun, good natured teasing of the women by the men as everyone tucked in to enough food to feed an army.

Elena dropped into a chair next to Marc who grabbed her to plant a hot kiss on the mouth.

"For the love of God, would you two stop with the lip-locks," Liam moaned.

"I think it's lovely," Nina said, digging a sharp elbow into Liam's ribs.

Liam pretended the elbow dig hurt.

Marc watched the by-ply between his sister and Elena's brother.

His eyes narrowed.

"I'm not sure Nina's old enough to handle your brother. How old is he anyway?" he muttered to Elena who was watching the way Liam whispered in Nina's ear, the words making the girl blush to the roots of her hair.

She patted Marc's cheek, twinkled into his eyes and gave him a smile a great white would be proud of.

"He's twenty-nine. Worry not. He's all talk."

Elena turned her attention on her brother, gave him a cheery grin.

"Marc's worried you'll lead Nina astray, Liam. I told him he's got nothing worry about. I told him about your no sex rule," she yelled to be heard over the noise.

The whole table went quiet as Daniel Kennedy looked at Liam and frowned.

"Rule?"

By Liam's look of utter confusion, it appeared he didn't know what Elena was talking about.

Excellent.

"Yeah, the promise he made to Jesus."

The Kennedy boys were regarding Liam's burning face with interest.

A pack of wolves were always quick to sense weakness in another.

"Elena," Liam said in a warning growl.

Her smile grew wider as she held his eyes and ignored the threat.

"What promise?" Adam wanted to know.

"The promise of celibacy," Elena said.

The whole table erupted in howls of derision as Liam sat back in his chair and folded his arms. He was not a happy bunny. But Elena wasn't finished, not by a long shot. She held up her hand for silence.

"Until marriage. Isn't that right Liam? Weren't you the one who told good old Tom that I had made a promise to Jesus to keep myself pure until I married?"

Her brothers now howled with laughter as Mary and Nina stared at Liam as if he'd grown two horns and a forked tail.

126

AN AFFAIR TO REMEMBER

The way Liam scowled at her, if looks could kill, Elena would be six feet under by now.

Ahh, Karma, Karma, you are such a bitch.

At her side, Marc choked on a Brussels' sprout and Joe helpfully banged his back.

"Liam?" Daniel Kennedy eyed his son. "Have you been sticking your nose into your sister's affairs... again?"

"When did this happen?" Adam wiped streaming eyes with his napkin.

"The night I had dinner at Ludlow Hall with Tom. The night Tom dumped me because of my 'no sex' rule. You might imagine my surprise, since I'd never heard of it."

Nina Jones now turned to give Liam big eyes.

"Really? You did that to your sister?"

Now Liam glared at Nina as if she was the enemy.

"I was only protecting her. Keeping her safe."

Nina turned her laughing gaze on Elena.

"How old are you again?"

"Twenty-six."

Nina sat back and stared at Liam for a couple of beats.

Liam wriggled in his seat.

"Seriously?" Nina said. "You do realise you have control issues?"

Liam turned to Marc.

"Help me out here. I bet you vet Nina's boyfriends, too?"

Marc shrugged.

"Nope. I trust her to use her common sense." Marc winked at his sister. "However, you might have done Elena a better favour by warning her of the dangers of After Shock."

Liam shook his head.

"Nah, Elena wouldn't touch the stuff, she's not got the head for it."

"You're telling me," Marc muttered, ignoring Elena's death stare.

Now Joe entered the fray as he grinned down the table at his baby sister.

"You did not drink After Shock. When did this happen?"

"The night we got together," Marc said, oblivious to a fiancée who kicked him under the table. "That was after the crazy guy who'd escaped from the psychiatric hospital and exposed himself to Elena in the restaurant. We had to restrain him. Then Tom dumped her. And then she decided to drown her sorrows with flaming After Shocks. It was a night to remember."

Elena realised there was a lot more to this relationship thing that met the eye. She'd need to have a little chat to her beloved about what happens at Ludlow Hall, stays at Ludlow Hall.

Nina just shook her head and gazed at Elena with something like admiration.

"Wow, never a dull a moment with you, is there?"

Elena topped up Nina's wine.

"You've got that right." Then she studied Nina's lovely face, the intelligence in her blue eyes. And the germ of an idea entered Elena's mind. "You're doing a communications and marketing degree?"

Nina nodded.

"I'm taking a sabbatical until mum's feeling better. Why?"

Elena took a sip of wine, watching Nina over the rim of the glass.

"How do you fancy doing a bit of work experience at Ludlow Hall? I've an opening in my department. Pay's good and it'll give you credits for your degree. What do you say?"

Nina's eyes flicked to her brother.

Marc nodded, turned to look at Elena. "Good thinking, and thank you."

"If you're absolutely certain you want me. I'd love to do it," Nina said.

Elena lifted up her glass and dinged it with a teaspoon, asking for order and silence.

"Merry Christmas!"

In response everyone yelled,

"MERRY CHRISTMAS!"

THE END

Not The End

Actually, it's not The End. It's just the beginning of a whole new off-shoot series to my Ludlow Hall series called Ludlow Nights. For more information and the first part of the story, HIS RULES, free, coming at the end of December in 2015 please sign up to my New Release newsletter at: **http://smarturl.it/ccmcksign**

You'll receive information on my new stories, deals and offers. Your contact details will not be shared with a third party and I promise not to spam your inbox.

Want to read where it all began? Reckless Nights In Rome is the stormy tale of how Nico and Bronte got together. It's the story that kicked off the Ludlow Hall series and the ebook is available everywhere FREE. Grab it now!

Reckless Nights in Rome - eBook 1 is FREE.

From my family to your family, MERRY CHRISTMAS!

Christine

Other Books in The Ludlow Hall Series
Available Now by CC MacKenzie

Reckless Nights in Rome - Book 1 (Free ebook)

A Stormy Spring - Book 2

Run Rosie Run - Book 3

The Trouble with Coco Monroe - Book 4

The Fall of Jacob Del Garda – Book 5

A Film Star, A Baby. and a Proposal Book 6

Delicious and Deadly: Invitation to Eden – Book 8

A Daddy for Daisy - Book 7 is due out in 2015

Keep in Touch on

Website
http://ccmackenzie.com/
Facebook
http://www.facebook.com/CCMzie
Twitter

AN AFFAIR TO REMEMBER

https://twitter.com/CCMacKenzie1
Email
ccmackenzie@ccmackenzie.com

Hear CC MacKenzie's latest news.
Interact with her Readers.
And Please leave a review.

Thank You!

Chapter One - A Film Star, A Baby, And A Proposal -

A Ludlow Hall Christmas Story
(Available Now)

The theme tune to the movie 'Jaws' swam through exhaustion to penetrate Matt's comatose brain.

He seriously hated that freaking music. Every time he heard it he got the heebie jeebies. And his agent damn well knew it. His hand slid out from under his pillow smacked the cell phone hard then tossed the big white to the floor. That was the second attempt to kill the shark this week. But just like the movie that bastard was hard to kill, and the music started up again, this time from somewhere under the bed.

He slung his arm over the side. Long fingers explored the glossy surface of solid oak until finally he gripped the cell and pulled it under the duvet.

"Unless someone's died, you're sacked," he growled.

"Har, har. I was about to tag Nico to see if Ludlow Hall had a famous dead person in the penthouse suite. Actually, if you were found dead the film would make even more moola."

With the duvet over his head, Mathias Carter groaned at the voice thundering in his ear, then yawned hugely. "It's nearly Christmas. Get a fucking life, Tobin."

"My wife, and yeah I *love* saying that so suck it up, says she had visions of you lying drowned in the bath."

"Bed," Matt grumbled and nuzzled deeper into his pillow. "In bed. Sleeping. Bye."

AN AFFAIR TO REMEMBER

"Hold it! Hold it right there, sunshine. I've sent you a surprise, something nice."

"Nope. Sleeping. Eighteen hour flight. Tired."

"The reviews of the film are stellar, pal. Stellar," Tobin said with something like glee.

In his head Matt could see his agent doing a bum boogie.

"Fucking don't care."

"Not to worry," his friend yelled in that permanent happy clappy voice he had these days. And Matt was genuinely pleased for him, he was. But all this falling in love shit was pitiful. It was spreading like flu. Every single one of his friends had been hit hard by the love bug. Dimly he heard Tobin continue, "I care enough for the both of us. The surprise will be there in an hour. Shake a leg, shave and shower."

"Yeah, yeah. Happy Christmas to Sophie for me."

Matt turned the phone to silent, tossed it on the floor, burrowed deep under the duvet and sank like a stone into the land of nod.

Excerpt - A Daddy for Daisy – Book 7
A Ludlow Hall Story
(Due 2015)

'Can She Find The Courage To Love Again?'

A Daddy for Daisy

Janine Faulkner is a woman who lives life by her own rules. After the death of her husband, she's thrown herself into raising her baby daughter, and then into her work as Chief Operating Officer for *Sweet Sensations*...

Janine likes life just as it is. She's not looking for love. Not even with gorgeous Joshua Erichsen, the Architect she hired to bring her family home, The Grange, back to life. His charm and ruthless good looks invade her every waking moment, but she's wary of a man who seems too good to be true...

Joshua Erichsen is drawn to the beautiful single mother right from the start. But Janine's past hides horrific secrets that have returned to haunt her... And it seems someone is determined to keep them apart, forever...

I learned that courage was not the absence of fear, but the triumph over it. The brave man is not he who does not feel afraid, but he, who conquers that fear.
NELSON MANDELA

AN AFFAIR TO REMEMBER

"Hey, how's my best girl?"

Joshua Erichsen crouched down to look into blue eyes that danced into his. Boo's little fists, wrapped in cute sheepskin mitts, batted his cheeks as he kissed her. The kid gave a happy laugh and blew bubbles from her tiny rosebud mouth. His eyes rose to the woman gripping the handles of the stroller and he didn't miss the way she'd gone absolutely still.

Shit.

He thought they'd gone past that. His eyes slid over the slim figure wrapped up in a quilted jacket the exact colour of her fabulous blue eyes. Those eyes met his and he recognised the usual wariness. As if he was the big bad wolf.

Six months ago, when he'd first met Janine Faulkner, he'd been attracted and intrigued. Then over time intrigue had morphed into irritation, and then from irritation into pissed off. A few weeks ago, they'd had a clearing of the air and things had been nice and friendly. So what the hell was her problem with him now?

What harm would it do, he wondered, to kiss that sulky mouth?

No. A pouting mouth, Josh decided. It was a mouth made for kissing. A mouth made for sucking his... Okay. Stop now.

But hell, she was an attractive woman. A beautiful woman, he corrected.

No matter how hard he tried, why couldn't he behave like a normal person around her? He didn't have a problem with woman. Women liked him. When he'd been with a woman, nobody got hurt, no harm, no foul. With a normal woman he'd do the little mating boogie, date once, twice, then the sex part of the deal. But Janine was not a normal woman. She had issues. She'd had a rough time. He got that. He did. With Janine he had as much chance of dating and mating as flying to the moon.

Dream on, sucker.

Janine wasn't interested. Worse, she was downright hostile if he even twitched in the wrong direction.

And why was he standing in front of her with his heart going boomdidiboom while she gave him a look that would melt solid steel? He didn't need this woman. A woman who was nothing but hard work. He didn't need the fucking hassle.

However, one female held his heart in her tiny fist and that female was one Daisy Boo Faulkner. Nearly eight months old and the light of his life. And the feelings were mutual because Boo adored him, too. And Josh knew that her daughter's love for him drove her mama crazy. However, she didn't do anything about it. And Josh reckoned that fact made Janine not only beautiful but a wonderful parent.

One day, he was sure, she'd make a lucky man a wonderful wife. And it would be a very lucky man to inherit that little ready-made family.

The pisser was it would never be him.

He whispered a curse and rubbed the ache that now lived in the back of his neck every time he was around her.

Josh rose and frowned as he took in Janine's pale face.

He admired her on so many levels. She was a fantastic mother. She worked hard and was doing an outstanding job running *Sweet Sensations*. Her friendship with Bronte and Rosie was deep and true. Granted she was a bit skittish around Nico Ferranti... and Josh Erichsen.

He sighed.

She was looking at him right now as if he was about to jump her bones.

If he was absolutely honest he'd been thinking a lot about perhaps dropping a little peck on her cheek to work his away, eventually, around to that fabulous mouth. But the Hand's Off sign was flashing in big red letters so he'd kept his distance.

She'd annoyed him.

Janine could tell by the way those Viking eyes cooled, the way his brows met, as if seriously puzzled and ticked off with her.

He was wearing a black ski cap, his blonde hair escaping here and there.

He stood and she found her head tipping back as she kept her eyes on his.

AN AFFAIR TO REMEMBER

He thrust his hands into the pockets of his black puffa jacket.

"Got time for a coffee?" he asked in a tone that dared her to refuse. He'd been using that tone a lot around her recently and her eyes narrowed, but before she could speak he continued, "Received the go ahead from planning for the new windows. So you need to make a choice of wood ASAP. I've brochures in the car."

In the early days he'd asked her out for dinner, twice, but she'd made it clear he was cocking his leg on the wrong tree. And that she was, Not Interested.

But for some reason today the challenge in those eyes annoyed her to the point where she raised her chin. Perhaps it was better that they discussed business in a public place. Perhaps her hormones would behave themselves around him for once.

"Okay. Where?"

He blinked and she didn't miss the surprise in his baby blues.

"Cafe Roma? They've Wi-Fi and I can show you a couple of amendments to the specifications for the kitchen."

Now irritation joined the lethal attraction that danced in her belly.

"I hope the amendments are not going to cost me."

His deep voice went soft and low. "I told you we're under budget. The amendments will save you money in the long run."

He was right, they were under budget. But it was okay for him, he didn't have responsibilities. Josh was financially solvent, single, footloose and fancy free. Plus, he had a very busy love life, if all the chit chat about him was to be believed.

Then she told herself that his love life was none of her business.

"Okay."

He walked next to the stroller and they stopped next to his big shiny black BMW parked at the curb to pick up his laptop and her brochures.

By the time Janine had settled Boo into a high chair with her bottle of water and a cookie, in Cafe Roma, Josh had returned to the table with a tray of frothy coffees and a collection of fresh muffins.

Irritation tickled the nerves jumping in her stomach.

She didn't *want* a muffin, Janine decided, happily forgetting she'd promised herself one of Bronte's later in the day.

"How much do I owe you," she asked in a tone that showcased her annoyance.

The way his eyes flashed and held hers as he tugged off his ski cap, unwound his cashmere scarf and shrugged out of his jacket made her belly twitch.

And Janine wished she'd kept her big mouth shut.

Under the jacket he wore a pale blue denim, button down shirt under a navy cashmere sweater. Matching jeans hugged muscled thighs and drew her eyes to a place she had no business looking. So her eyes kept on going down long, long, legs to the expensive boots of black leather. He wouldn't have looked out of place on an ad for GQ showcasing a man about town looking effortlessly gorgeous.

He sat and those eyes met hers as he placed a cup and saucer in front of her before taking muffins off the tray and then his own coffee, a jug of hot milk and a couple of bags of sugar.

"I'll add it to the bill," he said in a silky voice and placed a double chocolate chip muffin, the size of a man's fist, in front of her.

The way he assumed she'd do as she was told, like an obedient child, pressed a hot button.

Janine had never been a woman who went looking for an argument, she'd always been brought up to be polite and always to defer to the men in her life. It would have cost her nothing to say thank you and eat the goddamn muffin. But for some reason she just couldn't let it go.

"I don't believe I asked for a muffin."

Now those smooth brows rose.

"Don't want one? You could do with more meat on your bones."

Could she indeedy? And just who the *hell* did he think he was? She leaned over the table, into his face.

138

"I don't want a muffin. And my weight is none of your damn business."

Boo whimpered at her mother's tone and a flush of utter mortification burned up Janine's neck into her cheeks.

"Now look what you've done," Josh said in that horrible silky voice that made her want to belt him. "You've upset the baby."

Josh wanted to snap and snarl right back at her.

But the way her eyes filled as she soothed Boo and the way her hand shook as she stroked the baby's velvet cheek held him back.

She was upset over a muffin?

What. The. Fuck?

End of Excerpt "A Daddy for Daisy"

13738453R00083

Printed in Great Britain
by Amazon.co.uk, Ltd.,
Marston Gate.